Sophia and the Fisherman

A Romantic Mystery in the South of France

By

Fran Connor

Published by Liot Literary

© Fran Connor

Other novels by Fran Connor
The Devil's Bridge
Someone to Watch Over Me
Born to Blush
Passarinho and the Highlander
Her Man in Havana
Honourable Lies
Operation Hydra
The Genesis Project
The Alcazar Code
Dunkirk

Cover by MiblArt

1

CHAPTER ONE

Sophia pulled herself up to her full five feet ten inches; well three of them were the heels and gave the hapless check in guy a long stare with her startlingly green eyes. Then she put her fingers together and cracked the bones. Oh dear! This crack of the bones always heralded a storm like her own barometer. Finally, she took a deep breath. "I've told you already the name on the passport is my married name, Mrs Rattigan. I'm divorced and I haven't had time to change the passport," she hissed through her expensive teeth. "My secretary booked me in using the name I've reverted to, Ms MacDonald. Now please give me my boarding pass!" Sophia slammed her twenty-one kilo suitcase on to the conveyor belt and eyeballed the unfortunate young man again.

Shuffling and low mumbles from behind told Sophia the ever increasing queue was getting restless. She didn't care. She needed a holiday.

The stare did it. "All right Mrs Rat, er Ms Mac, er please get the passport changed before you travel again or use your married name." He shoved the necessary paperwork towards her. Sophia noticed he had ever such a slight tremble in his hand. She was used to that, making people tremble. "Just one more thing," muttered the clerk. "You are one kilo overweight on your luggage."

The stare.

"All right, I'll let it go this time."

Soon she was at thirty thousand feet looking down on a rare clear day over the English Channel. Far away from work pressures, far away from Charlie the Rat and looking forward to a couple of weeks in the South of France alone.

It didn't start well. The help desk man with a Gallic shrug promised to get her suitcase taken to her holiday address if it turned up. The stare hadn't worked. Much to her chagrin she had to admit these Frenchmen don't intimidate easily.

The taxi passed a landmark twice on the way from the airport. Sophia simmered close to boiling over. Why me, she asked herself? Her reasonable grasp of the French language couldn't help her understand the expletives the taxi-driver used when he dropped her off at her apartment and only received half of what he'd asked for. He understood her one finger gesture.

Sophia strolled around the apartment on the third floor of a three-storey building. She pushed open a sliding door to a balcony that looked out across the quaint old town towards the sea. The ozone reminded her of childhood beach holidays in Cornwall burying Dad in the sand while Mum clucked away with 'mind the sandwiches', 'be careful', 'put some more sunblock on'. Mum always knew best. She'd take the sandy sandwich herself so Dad and Sophia had the clean ones. She'd put the calamine lotion on Sophia's red body at night. Although Mum's 'I told you so' still rankled when Sophia finally told them last year about the divorce.

As she padded through a comfortably equipped living room, a painting of a chateau on the canary yellow wall over a fireplace drew her attention. It wasn't a huge chateau like those on the Loire. More of a place to live thought Sophia. On closer inspection, she saw the name of the place printed below, 'Chateau Mongaudon'. Sophia quickly dispensed with the daydream that crept into her head and checked out the American kitchen in the corner. Perfect, she thought but then wished she had someone to cook for.

In the hideous white and green distressed bedroom a huge iron bedstead with brass knobs nestled under a sloping roof. Sophia gave a deep sigh when she looked at the bed and felt a little sadness creeping in with the thought that she didn't have someone to share it with.

Impressionist prints of couples added to her gloom. The Degas print of 'The Absinthe Drinkers' brought a wry smile. Charlie the Rat and her in the last months of their marriage.

Sitting on the balcony in the warmth of the early summer evening Sophia sipped a chilled glass of Provencal Rosé while taking in the scent of the bougainvillea that tangled around the brickwork. Lights flickered way out to sea. Down below, she watched lovers walking and smelt the coffee from the bar next door.

Was this a good idea, she asked herself? Am I running away? The divorce had hit her hard. She'd been in turmoil since catching Charlie the Rat in their boat, in her bunk, on top of one his law students. She'd been unable to forgive him. It wasn't the first time. A quick divorce with the assets split down the middle and Charlie the Rat became history. It upset Sophia because he had cheated on her. That he wanted to cheat on her upset her even more. Was she getting old? Had she lost her allure? At twenty-nine was she too young for a midlife crisis?

Sophia finished the bottle of Rosé and made her way to bed.

Banging on the door woke her up. Through bleary eyes, she searched for the wall clock. Nine-thirty! Her dressing gown was in her suitcase wherever that may be so she threw on her clothes from yesterday and made her way to the door.

A young man stood there and smiled.

"Yes?"

"I 'ave your suitcase Madame."

"Great!"

And he heaved a suitcase from behind him.

"That's not mine!"

"But…"

"It isn't my suitcase."

"Are you sure Madame?"

"I bloody well know what my suitcase looks like. Oh sorry. It isn't your fault. Look, that isn't mine. Please take it back."

***

Shopping was never her favourite occupation. Was something genetically wrong with her? All her friends lived for shopping. Sophia hated it. A chore. So having to spend the first full day of her holiday traipsing around the shops for underwear, makeup and clothes because the stupid airline lost her luggage did not put her in a good mood.

The guy in the lingerie department at the big store. Would she hold that bra and pants against her so he could see what it would look like on his wife? Creep!

It didn't help when she used her credit card in the name of MacDonald and the shop assistant demanded identification. Again the long explanation over the passport before she could take her purchases away. An irritated Sophia stormed out of the store back to her apartment.

With a glass of wine, she sat on the balcony to unwind.

Sophia decided to treat herself to a meal out that evening and wandered along the quay until she found a little restaurant with tables and chairs outside, low music and a wonderful aroma from the kitchen.

Locals, not tourists, filled the other tables. An elderly couple waited for their food, no chat, not even a look at each other. Is that what happens, thought Sophia? Nothing to say? Two men in suits sat in deep discussion about the qualities of a lap dancing club somewhere nearby. A young couple gazed into each other's eyes. A chic woman fed her Pekinese with scraps from her plate. And Sophia sat there, alone, still wondering why she'd decided to come away on her own. Her friend Phillipa had offered to see if she could get time off and come with her, but Sophia had wanted to come alone though now she wasn't so sure.

An excellent meal made up for the lack of company. Sophia wolfed down the duck. She'd eaten in two-star Michelin restaurants. She'd never had one as good or as much of it in one go. The wine helped.

Replete with duck and wine she climbed into her lonely bed. As she reached for the bedside light to turn it off, Degas's masterpiece stared at her. The absinthe drinkers spent the night facing the wall.

She'd been up for an hour when she heard a door-knock.

The young man stood there again. He offered a suitcase. Sophia shook her head. He trundled away.

***

She'd liked the quayside and thought she'd take a look at in daylight.

Sophia delicately weaved her way along the grey concrete through fishermen's' nets piled high and lobster pots strewn with seaweed. A sweet smell of decaying sea creatures and tar wafted on the breeze. Her flowing red hair, flimsy white top, tight white cut-offs and espadrilles set off her figure attracting admiring glances from the fishermen. It boosted her ego until she realised none of them were exactly her idea of a romantic Frenchman.

"*Bonjour Madame,*" a reedy voice hailed from below the quay.

Sophia glanced down to see an ancient fisherman with a rope in a blue painted fishing boat. A small wheelhouse balanced on deck bobbed gently from the wake of a passing trawler. His stubble was definitely not designer and his blue jersey and flat cap were as old as he.

A second man wearing only a pair of sawn-off jeans stepped on deck from the wheel house. He had his back to Sophia, but his muscled bronzed torso and strong arms were clearly in view. A tattoo on his right forearm of a shield and two rampant lions drew her interest.

Turn round, turn round, Sophia silently pleaded but he lifted the hatch and climbed down out of sight without her catching a glimpse of his face. "Typical!" she uttered under her breath.

"*Sil vous plait!*" The ancient one threw the rope to her. Instinctively she caught it as she had done so many times for Charlie the Rat aboard their yacht.

"*Attachez la,*" the sailor called, pointing to a mooring post.

She deftly tied off the rope.

"*Merci*," called the fisherman. Sophia waved back to him and smiled as she decided to abandon any idea of waiting for muscles to come up for her perusal. After all, she thought, I'm only window shopping.

A huge white and rusty ocean-going trawler thrashed the water with its bow thruster and propeller as it shunted sideways towards the quay wall. The engines grumbled and spat blue smoke through the exhaust creating a light, stinking mist that drifted over the water to the dock to mingle with the shore odours.

Carefully she edged along the side of the dock to pass a row of crab pots and stole a glance over her shoulder to see if Mr Muscles had come back on deck. He hadn't, much to her disappointment. "Damn," she complained to herself and turned back too late to avoid tripping over a rope.

Head over heels, she fell until the cold water hit her warm body sucking the air from her lungs. Gulping for air, she kicked and struggled to the surface only to see the trawler bearing down on her. She screamed as she watched the trawler close on the quay with her as the meat in the sandwich. In seconds, she would be crushed, minced or both.

Suddenly she felt something drag her underwater. In the dark terror, she heard the throaty roar of the engines above and sensed the vortex from the propellers pulling her to her doom. But strong arms held her safe. She bobbed to the surface on the far side of the trawler. A head popped up beside her.

Her first impression was the eyes, as blue as the Mediterranean sky. Next she saw the sleek black hair with just a hint of grey at the temples suggesting an age of early thirties. A muscled arm with the shield tattoo took her by the shoulders and pulled her towards the ancient mariner's boat.

"*Mon Dieu*!" exclaimed the old man as he bent over the gunwales to pull Sophia aboard.

Shivering with fear and cold Sophia watched her rescuer climb on deck. She couldn't help her jaw-dropping when she saw this Adonis of the deep. An air of cool authority on the intelligent face rushed a warm feeling down through her body.

"I, I, I just don't know how to thank you," she blurted out.

"Laurent Mongaudon at your service Madame," said Adonis in a French accent that sent another feeling surging through her body making her blush. All thoughts of her recent close encounter with death evaporated under his gaze on her figure now plainly on view under the clinging, dripping clothes.

"Sophia MacDonald," she managed, trying to sound like the sophisticated woman she really was but it came out like a shy fifteen-year-old's introduction to the boy of her dreams.

"You may buy me dinner tonight Sophia MacDonald," said Laurent as he tugged a dirty coat from the wheel house and draped it over her shoulders.

The ancient Mariner rolled his eyes to the heavens and smiled to reveal one lone tooth.

Too flummoxed to put up even a token respectable resistance to the invitation she just nodded her head.

CHAPTER TWO

Sophia stretched her long legs as she sat on the balcony apartment among the bougainvillea and the geraniums. She sipped a well-earned, chilled Rosé. A lazy seagull circled in a thermal high above the harbour. Down below cars revved, people chatted, birds sang, but Sophia heard nothing as she fantasised of Laurent the Adonis making love to her until Charlie the Rat crept into her daydream.

"Damn," she said to the distant seagull. "I can't even dream now without him spoiling it."

The last three hours had been manic. First the hot bath to restore her senses. A rapid tidy of the already tidy apartment. Finally the sheets. She'd hesitated when she found herself changing the bed sheets. After all, she considered, was bed on a first date such a good idea? But she changed them anyway with a little shrug and a whimsical, well you never know! The absinthe drinkers got to see daylight again.

A quick glance at her Smartphone told her she had an hour to get ready. And she used every minute of it to fix her makeup and spray the perfume she'd bought to replace the more expensive one still in her suitcase. The loss also limited her choice of wardrobe, but she selected the stunning canary yellow dress she'd found in a little boutique the day before.

***

Laurent sat on a wall by the bridge over the canal watching a team of ants race to and fro from a dusty hole. He liked ants, their industry, their teamwork, their single-mindedness. He was pretty sure that they didn't have the worries that he had.

Sophia scurried into view only five minutes late. Laurent felt his heart skip a beat. It took all his willpower to keep his cool guy persona as she approached. What a transformation he marvelled, from the bedraggled woman he'd fished out of the harbour to this beautiful and elegant woman. He climbed to his feet; pastel blue linen jacket held with one finger over the shoulder of his white Polo shirt, the cotton straining to keep his muscled body in. His heart pumped like he'd just done a marathon. Laurent made women's hearts beat faster but what is this, he mused, she's doing it to me?

A smile creased his lips as she approached, now only six feet away and soon he would take in the scent of her body and her fragrant, lovely hair.

"Bonsoir," she chirped. Crack! "Aghhh!" Her three inch heel caught in a gap between the cobbles and snapped. The momentum threw her forward. In a panic to avoid a collision with her Adonis, she swished to the right only to catch him between the legs with her knee. He went down like a pack of cards holding his crown jewels.

She bent down and put her arms around him. He did indeed take in her perfume even recognising it as the same stuff he'd given Pascale for Christmas. "Damn," he said to himself. "I thought she would at least be a Chanel girl." Even so, Laurent knew that he'd happily crouch there for as long as she wanted to hold on to him.

She helped him to his feet. "I like to make an entrance."

Laurent's head stopped spinning and he judged it a good idea to let go of the injury.

Sophia slipped off the offending shoe. He took it from her like Prince Charming may have taken the lost slipper. He had no champagne so he just inspected it.

"Broken," he said. Off went his heart again when her gaze turned from the shoe to his injured area. "Only the shoe." They both dissolved into laughter. He snapped off the other heel so she could walk balanced.

The sun hung low but still had the warmth of a Mediterranean summer. Sweet fragrances from the flower tubs and baskets filled the air. Sophia's lungs felt fit to burst with the joy of being out on the town again with a man. And not just any man but this really cool guy.

"Where are we going?" She didn't really care as long he continued to guide her along the pavement with his arm around her shoulders. Her gait was a little awkward on the adapted shoes.

"I know a little place near 'ere"

Laurent held the back of her chair as they took their seats in a restaurant overlooking the harbour. His arm gently brushed her right breast causing her to let out an almost inaudible sigh, but his slight smile told her he'd heard it.

Blue linen covered the tables with matching chairs. It looked an expensive place, but Sophia didn't care even though she knew she was paying.

Like the genie from the lamp, a waiter in a DJ immediately appeared, nodded discreetly to Laurent and produced two red leather-bound menus.

"Anything you do not like?" His accent made it sound like a 'come to bed' and Sophia had to drag her thoughts back to eating. She shook her head. If he wanted her for dessert that was all right by her!

"Let me choose for you." He snapped his fingers and the waiter reappeared. "We'll 'ave the Fruits de Mer to start. Leave out the bulots. Then we will 'ave the pan-fried sea bass with that special jus that 'Enri makes."

The waiter nodded.

Laurent studied the wine list, "You still selling that stuff to the tourists?" He pointed at a Bordeaux red. "For that price! Shame on you!" He laughed and the waiter laughed with him. Sophia smiled when she remembered how many times London restaurants had ripped her off over the wine bill.

Eventually, having run back and forth through the wine list he settled on a white burgundy. Sophia managed to glimpse the price. Bloody hell, she thought, forty-eight euros and I'm paying!

The waiter vanished like the genie.

"Bulots?"

"I think you call them whelks and I doubt you like them."

"I hate them," answered Sophia but it wasn't the taste, it was the memory of Charlie the Rat gorging himself on them when he took her to Blackpool. She wished he could see her now sitting in this beautiful town in the south of France with, without a doubt, the sexiest man she had ever met.

Laurent poured the wine. She was no wine buff. Something special or just his presence? She didn't care.

A huge dish bore the 'Fruits de Mer'; mussels, clams, crab, prawns, langoustines and other strange creatures that Sophia had never seen before. She realised she shouldn't have put the yellow dress on.

Laurent had no such worries. He tucked in using his crab spike and crackers like it was his first meal in days. She marvelled at his well-manicured fingers, so out of place in a fisherman. And, dammit, far nicer than her own. Her temperature rose as she imagined those same hands touching her body. His expert tongue extracting the last of the juice from the crab claw gave her visions of ecstasy.

Sophia managed to finish her share of the seafood with only a little splash of prawn on her dress.

The two sea bass that arrived were so big that Sophia cracked a joke that they could feed the five thousand with them. Laurent didn't understand.

"Ow could two of these feed five thousand?"

Oops, thought Sophia, Adonis has an Achilles heel, he hasn't got a sense of humour or he's just thick.

She opened her mouth to try to dig herself out when she saw the twinkle in his eye. The grin spread on his face and then he let out a sexy chuckle as he stared into her green eyes. Fortunately, her legs turning to jelly didn't matter as she was sitting down.

To regain her composure she gazed out at the twinkling harbour lights. The sun had dipped over the horizon and the night enfolded them but still the heat of the day hung on the flower-scented air.

The wine and the food helped Sophia to relax and emboldened her at the same time. "Why is a man like you working on a fishing boat?"

"What's wrong with being a fisherman?"

"Well, nothing. Really you don't strike me as being a fisherman."

"What do I strike you as?"

She smiled. "Oh, I don't know. Perhaps a ship's captain, a soldier or the boss of a big company." Or a sheikh who wants to drag me back to his tent and make passionate love to me, she fantasised.

Now he was looking into her slightly open mouth. "I'm a simple man with simple needs." Unashamedly he turned his gaze to her breasts straining beneath the canary yellow. But she sensed it wasn't a leer like you get on the Underground or in pubs. No, his look appeared altogether different, not threatening, not even embarrassing. He had a hunger in those eyes, a desire for her she thought, she hoped.

"There's something enigmatic about you. Tell me, who are you really?"

"I'm Laurent Mongaudon, fisherman. Now tell me who Sophia MacDonald is."

Mongaudon? Mongaudon? Sophia ran the name through her brain. She'd seen that name somewhere but couldn't place it. "I run a company that makes furniture, isn't that interesting?" She took a sip of wine still pondering the name Mongaudon.

"You don't wear a wedding ring but are you married? Have a partner? A lover?"

"Divorced, single and unattached!"

"Oh, I'm sorry."

"So was I but I'm not now." Sophia looked straight back into his blue eyes. He smiled and her legs went to jelly again.

A stroll through the old streets, now a little cooler in the evening air, took them through a fountain square. He dipped his hand into the water and rubbed it against his neck. She longed for that hand to caress her.

Laurent sat Sophia on the edge of the fountain and stood in front of her. He looked so tall and attractive standing there in front of her that she, for the first time in her life, felt in awe of another human being. This guy had something, something she couldn't fathom. If he was a poor fisherman, she would be happy to be his fishwife.

He leant forward and his lips gently brushed her own. She closed her eyes waiting for the next one. It didn't arrive. She opened them and caught a glimpse of Laurent for an instant looking slightly uncomfortable. Was he shy? The thought made her legs turn to jelly again and set off enough butterflies in her tummy that she could have floated away on their beautiful wings.

"Shall we take a walk along the beach?" Laurent pointed towards a lighthouse half a mile down the coast.

Sophia would rather have walked to her apartment, dragged Laurent inside and made passionate love to him. "If you like."

They strolled barefoot through the sand, still warm from the day's heat. Laurent on the outside exuded cool but deep within he felt the struggle. "Don't do it!" The voice of reason begged. He'd fallen for her. Found himself lost in the green eyes of this gorgeous woman alongside him. Lost in the fragrance of her hair. Lost in her perfume even if it wasn't Chanel.

Suddenly, a huge Dobermann appeared from under a beached rowing boat. A deep throaty snarl came from its open jaws as it sized them up. Sophia usually had no fear of dogs. Where she lived, the dogs were rat-sized and walked by fur-coated women. She didn't like this one.

Laurent pulled Sophia behind him. He stepped forward. The dog stood its ground, vicious teeth exposed and saliva around the jaws. Another step forward by Laurent, now the dog took a couple of steps forward.

Another step forward by Laurent and two more by the dog had Sophia's heart in her mouth. The Dobermann bounded the gap and rolled over.

Laurent tickled its tummy. "Don't frighten people like that Peppi," he laughed.

Sophia had something of a sense of humour failure but quickly managed to regain control.

On they strolled to her apartment. This is it, mused Sophia, so glad I changed the sheets.

She tried a nonchalant, "Would you like to come in for coffee?"

Laurent took her in his strong arms and kissed her long on her lips. She felt his strong body pressed hard into hers. "Thanks," said Laurent. "But I sail early tomorrow." And off he went.

Sophia gazed wistfully at the lost opportunity. But she had the comforting knowledge that what she had felt against her in the kiss showed that he had wanted her. She hoped he'd come back to claim what was freely, openly and unashamedly on offer.

"Wow!" she said out loud after he disappeared around the corner.

CHAPTER THREE

Sophia awoke to a bright sunny morning and threw back the shutters to look out over her view. Fishing boats bobbed to and fro with their slippery cargoes while the pungent aroma of coffee filtered up from the café next door. She wondered if Laurent would ever come back into her life.

A knock at the door snapped her out of her dreaming. Remembering just-in-time to pull on some clothes she opened the door ready for disappointment by the wrong luggage again. Only this time it wasn't the boy from the airport. An enormous bouquet of flowers with every colour in the rainbow filled the door frame. A hand emerged with an envelope. Sophia took the envelope and then the flowers. The sixteen-year-old delivery boy, now revealed, sighed with relief and staggered off down the stairs.

Almost bursting with excitement, Sophia put the flowers on her dining table and ripped open the envelope.

"Dear Sophia, I have to go to the Camargue tomorrow on business. It will only take me a couple of hours and the rest of the day we can spend sightseeing if you would care to join me. I'll pick you up at eight o'clock. Laurent Mongaudon."

A smile spread across her face until it was ear to ear. She breathed in the sweet scent of the flowers. There's that name again 'Mongaudon'. She looked at the painting of the chateau on the wall. "Mongaudon, that's it," and rushed over to the picture to check. 'Chateau Mongaudon' there was no doubt about it. Wait a minute, she reasoned. I knew a guy called Alan Buckingham, but he lived in a grotty South Kensington basement flat, not the palace.

***

Laurent arrived on time. She'd been up for two hours ringing the changes with her limited wardrobe before finally settling on a pair of tight white cut-offs and powder-blue top. She accessorised with a silky red scarf and set the whole thing off with white slip-ons. They wouldn't be much good for hiking, but boy were they the bees knees in footwear. They should be. She'd forked out a three-figure sum at the boutique for them.

Sophia looked down from her balcony to see him waiting in a new deep blue cabriolet, roof down, with white leather seats. Not the car, she thought, that a humble fisherman would be driving. She threw him a wave, he blew a kiss back and she ran down the stairs to the street below.

Laurent climbed out of the car, stretched up to his full six feet one and smoothed down his white collarless cotton shirt that clung to his manly chest like a limpet to a rock. He kissed her twice on each cheek, opened the passenger door and handed her in.

Away they went along the boulevards and streets. Soon they were on the open road with plane trees both sides and field after field of grapevines. The fortunate choice of the scarf saved Sophia's hair from disaster.

"Nice car, is it yours?"

"No. Belongs to a friend. Mine is in the body shop. Stopped at a stop sign. The idiot behind didn't."

"Yeah, I've seen how some of these Frenchmen drive."

"Actually it was a woman."

"Perhaps you shouldn't have stopped so suddenly."

"Sister solidarity?"

And they both laughed.

"So what business is this you're doing if you don't mind me asking?"

"Beautiful around here isn't it?"

Okay, thought Sophia. He's obviously cagey about what he does so let's just go with the flow. Probably something to do with fish.

Soon they were in the flat, watery landscape of the Camargue, unlike anything she knew in Britain and a far cry from the urban sprawl of London. Flamingos balanced precariously with their beaks in the water. Overhead a massive flock of geese made its way in a V formation. The sun burned down. The insects buzzed. And all was well in Sophia's world.

Laurent braked suddenly as a white horse bolted from the reeds across the road. Sophia was utterly spellbound by the beauty around her, inside as well as outside of the car.

The car pulled into a gateway. The rusted gates lay like broken ribs on the parched earth. Sophia saw a scruffy stone building among the lime trees. A notice above the door advertised the 'Café du Lac'. Empty bottles filled a rack by the side of the building. A fat man in his sixties, huge moustache and denim jeans sat on the veranda in a fug of tobacco smoke. A younger man, skeletal, with a nose Cyrano de Bergerac could have worn sat picking it opposite the fat man.

Laurent stopped the car, reached into the glove box and pulled out a shiny automatic pistol. Sophia's eyes widened in terror. Gun crime was a constant nightmare around where she lived. This was the last place she expected to confront it. Laurent leapt from the car, strode across the yard and vaulted the fence to land on the veranda.

He stuck the gun in the wobbly double chin of the fat man. Terror began to creep into her; she looked down at her hands to see them shaking. She took a deep breath. She'd stuck up for herself against the mindless idiots who plagued her local streets and she wasn't going to let this gangster rattle her, however good he looked!

The skeleton dashed into the building and dashed back out carrying a bundle of euros. He counted out a pile and shoved them at Laurent. Pocketing the euros, Laurent removed the gun from fat man's chin, leant over and whispered into his ear.

Sophia's sheer determination would stop her being taken as a gangster's squeeze who had just knocked over a café for the takings, she hoped.

Laurent climbed back into the car. He drove off in a cloud of dust leaving the fat man and the skeleton on the veranda decidedly unhappy but not nearly as unhappy as Sophia.

"What the hell do you think you are doing?" demanded Sophia angrily overcoming her fear.

Laurent glanced sideways at her and smiled. No jelly legs this time, just sheer anger as Laurent pulled off the road next to a cottage wrapped in Virginia creeper. Before she could grab his shirt, he was out of the car.

An old woman dressed in black and with a face like leather tended her tomatoes. She looked up and waved at Laurent. Sophia sat in the car with her arms folded tight across her body, still seething. She watched as Laurent pulled the wad of euros from his pocket and handed it to the old woman. She kissed his cheek. From her apron pocket, she produced a cheroot and stuck it in her mouth.

Laurent drew the gun from his other pocket and pointed it at her face. She didn't budge or tremble, just stood there ready. Sophia closed her eyes as she saw the finger close on the trigger. She'd be a witness to a murder. Perhaps even an accessory. Did they still have the guillotine in France?

"Oh my God!" she cried as she covered her ears. But she didn't hear a bang. Opening her eyes, she saw Laurent lighting the cheroot for the old woman from the barrel of the gun.

"That does it!" said Sophia out loud to nobody. "A toy gun."

Laurent climbed back into the car and off they went again swerving as Sophia beat him about the head and shoulders.

"Stop this car now! Tell me what the hell is going on!"

Laurent pulled into a track by a row of lime trees. He smiled. "She's the wife of the fisherman I work with. Those crooks at the café swindled 'er out of two thousand euros last week just because they could. I got it back for 'er."

"But they'll call the police. They think you're armed. The gendarmes will shoot us down!"

"They won't call the police. Too many questions they'd 'ave to answer." Laurent smiled.

Now she realised she wasn't with public enemy number one she visibly relaxed. "Robin Hood!" she joked.

"Not really." Sophia detected just a slight sign of embarrassment which melted her heart.

She leant forward and kissed him gently on the lips. He looked surprised but quickly responded pressing his lips tightly against hers. His tongue searched for a way through and she parted her lips to receive it.

She felt his hand slip under her top. She hadn't 'done it' in a car since she was eighteen and this Cabriolet wasn't exactly designed for the purpose but, "Who cares?" she said to herself.

In the distance came the distinct sound of a tractor.

"Just my luck," said Sophia disentangling herself from his arms as the tractor rumbled into view along the track ruining the moment.

Laurent deftly handled the car along the narrow lanes always able to anticipate the suicidal tendencies of the local wildlife. They arrived at their lunch destination without contributing to the extinction of any species.

He was out of the car in a jiffy holding the passenger door open for Sophia to alight. He handed her down from her seat. Laurent gave her hand a little squeeze and his heart missed a beat. "You shouldn't have done it," he heard his conscience complain. "You'll be sorry, and more to the point, she'll hate you for it." But Laurent had been smitten.

He chose a veranda table at the restaurant. A view looked over the flat landscape of the Camargue. A wild place. Sophia had read about it as a child. A land of white horses, water and romance. And now she was here with *him*!

It didn't look expensive, the restaurant, but Sophia realised that on a fisherman's pay it would make a sizeable hole in Laurent's budget. She knew that all French restaurants had to provide a set price lunch menu during the week and so she chose from that rather than the 'a la carte'.

"Are you sure that's what you want?" asked an incredulous Laurent after the waitress had taken their orders and disappeared inside.

"Why? What's wrong with what I ordered?"

"I'm not sure you'll like tripe sausages."

"Oh sh…"

"I'll get you the Dorade!" And off he hurried in pursuit of the waitress.

Two hours later, full of fish and crème brulèe, Sophia called the waitress over. She wasn't sure how she was going to do this without causing embarrassment to Laurent. She didn't want him going hungry for the rest of the week by having to pay. But Laurent took the bill and pulled out a few dog-eared notes from his pocket and laid them on the table. She knew not to make a fuss for his sake and thanked him profusely for the meal.

Like two furtive lovers they spent the afternoon ostensibly looking at the scenery and wildlife but all the time searching out that quiet little spot where they could at last make love. Well, that was Sophia's motive and she hoped it was his too although they hadn't actually discussed it.

It didn't happen. They'd come close. In a wooded cove, a troop of Boy Scouts on a nature ramble found the cabriolet more interesting than the flamingos.

The three glasses of water Laurent drank with his lunch after a while meant he had to find a suitable place to get rid of them. He pulled over and disappeared into a clump of bushes.

Curiosity overcame Sophia. She lifted the catch on the glovebox to take a peek at the 'gun'. It lay on a small blue folder that had a green paper protruding. She could just make out 'Pascale Mongaudon' typed in what looked like the address box of an insurance certificate. A lipstick and a compact lay behind the gun.

Out of the corner of her eye, she spotted Laurent making his way back to the car. She slammed the glove box shut.

Athletically he jumped into the car and gave Sophia a big smile. When she didn't smile back, he raised his eyebrows. "What?"

"Who owns this car?"

"Why?"

"Who is Pascale Mongaudon? Your wife?"

It hit Laurent like a kick in the guts. "Told you," said his conscience.

"No, she isn't my wife." He wasn't lying, at least not at this stage. "We share a great-grandfather. I think that makes her a distant cousin or something."

"Why do you have her car?"

"I told you, mine is in for repair."

"Very generous of her to lend you this one."

"We're good friends. Look, Pascale is in a 'appy relationship with someone. She lives in Paris most of the time but keeps her car 'ere because she doesn't need it there. She visits me quite often. She likes it 'ere. And she comes with her boyfriend." Sophia saw his breathing increase, his outward cool gone. Was he lying?

A sour atmosphere pervaded the car on the drive back to Sophia's apartment.

Sophia watched the huge sun disappear into the far off underworld leaving the whole western sky ablaze in an orange glow. So many of her favourite paintings, the ones she painted and the ones she liked to see in galleries, had the setting sun as their subject. Perhaps it was melancholia; perhaps the sun was setting on this romance before it even started, thought Sophia.

Laurent pulled the Cabriolet into the side of the road outside Sophia's apartment. She climbed out. "Thank you for a nice day," she said and quickly went indoors.

CHAPTER FOUR

Sophia awoke the next morning with that horrible feeling of being in the wrong. She'd given Laurent a hard time without any real evidence to suggest that he deserved it. Had she blown the chance of a great romance? Maybe he was too good to be true and they say, she tried to convince herself, that if it looks too good to be true then it probably is. But no, that feeling inside told her she'd been stupid. She'd have to enjoy her holiday without him.

Or would she? If I could find him and apologise? Yeah? You? Apologise? Who are you kidding?

A knock on the door broke her internal wrangle. She opened it with hope in her heart. Had he come back for her? The bad news was the luggage boy stood there. The good news was that he had the right suitcase.

Sophia unpacked her belongings. Her stunning little black dress sent a lump to her throat. How Laurent would have liked her in that!

She wandered along the quay careful not to fall in. Neither Laurent nor the funny little fishing boat with its ancient mariner could be seen.

Sophia dined alone at the restaurant where she'd enjoyed the evening with Laurent. A different waiter served her. The one from her other night there must have had the night off. The food tasted nowhere near as good it had before and she was glad to finish and make her way back to her lonely apartment.

For three days she moped around the town ever optimistic of running into him but without success. She couldn't find him in the phone book. She couldn't find him anywhere.

On the fourth day, Sophia awoke to a commotion in the street below. She peeked out from the balcony in her bra and pants to see the whole town decked out in bunting and stalls selling just about anything you may wish to buy.

Now she had her suitcase and belongings she decided to dab a little of her good perfume behind her ears. A quick breakfast of yogurt and toast and she dashed down among the mayhem.

With her bag full of three T-shirts, a pair of espadrilles, two dried sausages and a bottle of Provencal Rosé Sophia made her way back to the apartment.

"Bonjour," a voice behind her purred. And there he stood: Adonis from the deep. Laurent in all his manly glory.

"Oh!" Sophia could have kicked herself for not coming up with something better than 'Oh!'

"I'm so sorry, I would 'ave come sooner but I 'ad to go away on business," said Laurent.

Jelly legs again for Sophia. "Well you're here now and I must apologise for my behaviour the other day," said Sophia not a little surprised to hear herself in the apologetic tone.

"Drink?"

"Why not?" said Sophia.

Laurent took in her scent. "Chanel?"

"Yes."

"I thought so. Suits you well."

Sophia felt so grateful that her belongings had arrived.

He led her through the throng to a little bistro up an alleyway with seats out on the pavement. She had a 'café au lait' and he had an espresso. They sat, a little awkward at first but soon they were comfortable again in each other's company.

"What 'ave you been doing?"

"Not a lot," she replied. Well, she wasn't going to tell him that she'd been searching the town for him.

Laurent took a deep breath. He wasn't good at this. Knowing what you want to say and saying it were two different things he understood too well. But this woman

38

he hardly knew owned his beating heart. He must go for it or forever regret the lost opportunity. "Please don't take this the wrong way," he began. "I'd like to invite you to my 'ome to spend a few days if that is all right with you?" There, he'd said it. Now he waited eagerly for the response.

The response was a blank stare.

"Arghh!" he uttered almost audibly. "Too forthright." Laurent took another deep breath and looked into Sophia's green eyes. "What I mean is, what I want to say is, would you like to come back to my 'ouse where I 'ave a spare bedroom and you will be perfectly safe. I will behave like a proper gentleman. There is a lock on the bedroom door, and…"

Sophia put her finger to his lips. "Yes, I'd love to come."

"You'll be sorry!" Laurent heard his conscience say.

At the agreed time, Laurent arrived to collect Sophia from her apartment. This time he wasn't in the cabriolet. She watched him from her balcony park a Citroen Safari in the street below and jump out. Sophia didn't know about cars. She knew this one was a sixties throwback in beautiful condition. She eagerly waited as she heard the footsteps on the stairs.

A knock on the door and she knew it wouldn't be the luggage boy this time. Sophia opened the door. He took her in his arms and kissed her gently but long on the lips. No continental kiss on the cheeks this time thought a relieved Sophia.

He carried her heavy suitcase down the stairs like it contained feathers. She tagged on behind full of hope and excitement. She'd not been this happy since, well, she didn't know when.

"Nice car," she said as he handed her into the passenger seat of the gleaming beige limousine with its white velour interior.

"Restored it myself," he replied proudly as he climbed into the driver's seat.

A bench seat in the front noted Sophia. Saves getting in the back she thought with a wicked giggle inside. And worth a lot of money. Perhaps that's how he supplements his fishing income, she mused. She hoped his humble little cottage nestled in a quiet backwater somewhere and they'd spend a few precious days, and with a bit of luck, nights, together in a rural idyll.

Soon they were whisking their way through the vineyards and ancient villages until at last, after about half an hour, he slowed down and stopped by a pair of heavy wrought iron gates.

Sophia looked up. Her jaw fell open. She couldn't believe it. There beside the gates hung a sign 'Chateau Mongaudon'. In the distance, at the end of a long drive, stood the chateau in the painting. Sophia, for once in her life was utterly speechless.

The car gently rolled along the drive making a hissing noise over the gravel until it finally stopped before the grand building. A fountain gushed from a Greek goddess into a magnificent marble basin and roses bloomed everywhere.

Opening the car door for Sophia, Laurent made a bow, "Welcome to my humble home my lady!"

The only reply she could muster was an inadequate, "Wow".

Down the steps and up to Laurent bounded a Dalmatian which then ran round and round him barking until it finally raised itself on its hind legs and put its paws on his shoulder. "Napoleon!" laughed Laurent as he lowered the dog.

Bertrand, a silver-haired distinguished looking man of about sixty in a dark suit and green apron, glided down the steps. He bowed to Laurent, "Bienvenue Monsieur Le Comte." Laurent gently patted him on the shoulder.

"Monsieur Le Comte? You're a count? Shi… I mean, really?"

CHAPTER FIVE

Bertrand unloaded the luggage from the Citroen. Laurent guided Sophia up the steps and into a vast entrance hall. She counted three wild boar heads, two stags and a surprised looking bear's head hanging on the oak panelled wall among a veritable armoury of pikes, swords and muskets.

Two staircases, one running to the left and one to the right climbed from the far end of the hall. Sophia saw a magnificent carving of a shield and two rampant lions on the wall where the stairs separated. She looked at Laurent's arm to see the same image.

Sophia grabbed hold of Laurent and spun him around to face her. "Tell me Laurent, who the hell are you?"

"Comte Laurent Dominique Nicolas 'Enri De Mongaudon, fisherman and a few other things."

"I thought the aristocrats lost their heads in the revolution?"

"Not the smart ones!" He put his finger under her chin, raised her head and kissed her softly.

"I don't have the right clothes for this place."

"What makes you think you'll need clothes." He raised an eyebrow. "In the bedroom you are using there is a selection of items belonging to my cousin. She won't mind if you borrow them."

He took her hand and guided her up the stairs, past portraits of stern-looking men and even sterner looking women. On the first floor landing stood a bronze head and shoulders of a soldier. "Great, great, great-grandfather fought with Napoleon in Egypt and Russia. 'E died at Waterloo. Those English!"

Sophia steeled herself to retort to this insult of her country when she saw a slow smile inch across his lips.

Along the carpeted corridor, they came to a massive ornate door. Laurent reached for the door handle and turned it. He took Sophia by the elbow and led her into the spacious chamber. A canopied bed stood against one wall with a view out across the immaculate grounds. Fresh flowers stood in a vase on an Empire style table. Sophia imagined Marie Antoinette would have felt at home in this room.

Laurent pulled open a wardrobe door to reveal a vast array of high couture. Sophia recognised some of the labels. She wasn't poor, but she'd never had a wardrobe like this one.

Laurent smiled happily. "'Elp yourself to anything you wish."

Sophia knew she had to handle this a lot more carefully than she'd bungled the challenge to him over Pascale's car. "Oh my they are beautiful. However did you amass such a collection?"

"Well of course they're not mine. Of my many idiosyncrasies, cross-dressing isn't one of them. They belong to Pascale, she keeps them 'ere as there isn't enough room in her Paris apartment."

There's that name again. Pascale. A distant cousin. Hmmm. Don't make a fuss. "Shame she has all this here and lives in Paris where she could wear it." Sophia wanted to know exactly what Pascale's status was in the chateau and more to the point, with Laurent.

"Don't worry, she 'as an excellent collection up in Paris," said Laurent oblivious to the subtle probe.

"How often does she come down here? I mean, does she have much chance to wear these clothes?

"Yes, she visits when she can. That's why she keeps a car 'ere."

"What would she say if she knew I was here?"

"She knows. I phoned her earlier to ask if it was all right for me to put you in 'er bedroom and perhaps wear a couple of 'er things. She's 'appy with that."

"Hmmm."

"And when she does come she brings her boyfriend with her! Perhaps boyfriend is the wrong word. He must be twenty years older than she is. Still they've being seeing each other for nearly two years now." Laurent took both of Sophia's hands in his, raised them to his lips and kissed them gently.

"Sorry!" Sophia heard herself say.

"And they're coming down in a couple of weeks. Which reminds me, how long can you stay?"

"Trying to get rid of me already?"

"Not at all. I'd like you to stay forever."

Sophia felt he actually meant it and the butterfly tummy kicked in. She'd have to make some decisions soon.

Laurent left her to unpack and sort out what she wanted to wear for dinner that evening. At least he'd given her a clue. Black tie. She must find something suitable.

After rummaging through her own things and the evening dresses in the wardrobe, she settled on a stunning full-length white dress. "Makes you look like a bride, virginal," said Sophia to her reflection in the mirror as she held the dress against her jeans and T-shirt. Quickly she dismissed the memory that crept into her mind, a memory of the wedding dress she'd worn when she married Charlie the Rat. If she'd known what it would be like she could have saved herself years of heartbreak.

Sophia wondered where the bathroom could be. Laurent, typical guy, hadn't told her. She opened a door in the wall opposite the bed to find an enormous bathroom. Centre stage stood an immense bath on clawed feet with antique style taps. She looked across to the far corner to see a capacious shower cubicle. A wash basin with antique taps and a large mirror above stood to the side of a window. A makeup mirror on the lip of the bowl was a nice touch, she thought.

She padded across the black-and-white tiled floor to the sash window to smell the fresh flowers on the sill. He'd thought of everything.

Sophia finished her makeup. She'd spent a very long time creating the face that she wanted to show. Expensive lessons her Dad had paid for when she left school ensured she knew exactly how to use her assets to the best. She stood in front of the wardrobe full-length mirror. Her first look startled her. "Who's that?" she purred to herself. "Me! Wow!"

A knock at the door filled her with excitement. If Charlie the Rat could see her now! She crossed the parquet floor with a click click of her heels to find Laurent at the door, dressed in a white tuxedo and every inch the debonair gentleman. If they were looking for a new James Bond, she mused, they could do no better than hire Laurent.

He led her down the stairs to a terrace at the back of the chateau. Sophia sipped champagne as she looked out on the perfect gardens and landscape as beautiful as any she'd seen in her world travels.

"Excuse me for a moment." Laurent disappeared into the chateau leaving her to gaze at the wonders and marvel at her luck. Napoleon the Dalmatian chased a red squirrel up a tree and ran around the bottom until he finally gave up and lolloped off to find another victim to annoy.

"Sorry about leaving you alone," said Laurent as he strolled across the terrace with the champagne bottle in his hand.

They wined and dined in the splendour of the dining room with its own cut-glass chandelier, mahogany everywhere and a table set with silver on a white linen tablecloth that she felt must be an expensive antique. Bertrand served attentively while Sophia in her white dress that was slightly too tight around her chest, tummy and bum soaked in the sheer luxury of her surroundings and the excitement of Laurent's company. He looked so distinguished in his white tuxedo that little ripples ran through her body.

A mosquito landed on his neck. He slapped it. "Those damned things."

"Me too. Had to have all sorts of injections before I went to the tropics to make sure that I didn't catch anything. The worse though was the malaria tablets. Made me ill."

"Well, we don't have malaria here, just damned 'ungry mosquitoes."

The first course she recognised as foie gras lightly fried with apple and served on a piece of toast. She picked at it, ate the apple and toast and left the foie gras.

"Not to your liking?"

"I'm sorry." Again this apologising she thought. Why the hell am I sorry? They torture the poor goose to death and eat its liver!

"Excuse me." Laurent rose from the table, left his napkin in his place and strode out of the dining room. Bertrand followed.

Sophia stood up and wandered around the dining room. At the far end of the room, a grand piano stood like its name suggested, grandly. Odd, she thought as she fingered the inscription 'Steinway', a house this size should have a music room of its own.

She perched on the stool and lifted the lid off the keys. Sophia couldn't resist when she saw the ebony and ivory. The room filled with the music of Chopin just as Laurent came back.

"You play so well," he purred. She smiled. Expensive makeup lessons weren't the only thing Daddy had paid for.

Sophia lowered the lid and glided back to her place at the table.

In her gap year before university, she'd travelled far and tasted many exotic foods. She'd never tried the next course before. So when Bertrand brought snails, a dozen of them for her, she flinched not least because she had no idea how to eat them.

"They're nothing like bulots, er whelks," he comforted. "Like this." He took hold of a silver clamp like device and lifted a snail from her plate then inserted a thin pronged pick to pull out the garlic butter covered occupant. Laurent leant forward and gently put the snail into her mouth.

"Mmm, tasty," she said honestly. Sophia tucked into the rest of her snails. No conscience troubling her in eating these little beauties.

A pink sorbet arrived next. She couldn't quite identify the subtle taste she picked up. "Made using Provencal Rosé," said Laurent.

"My favourite wine."

"Yes, I know."

Ten out of ten for observation Sophia had to admit.

"So, how long are you staying?" Laurent smiled at her as Bertrand served the main course, calf's liver in a thick brown sauce with a couple of carrots on the side.

"I should be going back next week but I think I can extend it if I can have access to a computer. There's some work I need to do." Sophia picked at the liver.

"You don't like it? You're a vegetarian?"

"No, but I expect this poor calf was kept in a cage and slaughtered before it had a life, sorry," apologised Sophia yet again. She ate the carrots.

The cheese course didn't cause her any alarm and as she helped herself to a mature Roquefort her gaze fell on a portrait of a young man and woman on the wall behind Laurent. Their hairstyle and clothes suggested the late sixties or early seventies era. The man looked a lot like Laurent.

"Who are they?" asked Sophia.

"My mother and father."

"Where do they live?" Sophia asked cutting another slice of the salty Roquefort.

"Father died ten years ago, heart attack. That's why I've in'erited the estate. Mother never really got over it. She died about three years ago. Broken 'eart I would say," said Laurent with what Sophia detected as a slight dampness about his wonderful eyes.

She reached out for his hand and squeezed it. "Sorry!" For goodness sake stop saying sorry, her inner self complained.

"My Mum and Dad are somewhere out in the Pacific. He retired last year. They're sailing around the world. I took over the business, but he keeps an eye on me."

"Sailing around the world? You mean on their own boat or on a cruise?"

"Their boat. He knows what he's doing."

"Impressive. Sounds like a man I would like to meet."

"Don't forget, he's not doing it alone. Mum is helping him."

"Quite a family!"

Dessert arrived and was just about the best crème brulée that Sophia had ever tasted.

"So, who cooked all this?"

"The cook!"

"You have your own chef?"

"Doesn't everybody?"

"I must get the recipe from him."

"How do you know it is a 'im?"

"So you have a woman looking after your needs down in a basement somewhere?"

"Maybe," he laughed.

Sophia looked at Bertrand standing quietly by the wall. Just the faint trace of a smile seemed to cross his lips.

Perhaps, she thought, there's some private joke I'm excluded from here. But it didn't dent her happiness in the slightest even though she'd baulked at the idea of eating cruelly raised animals.

"Now I know your English reservations about food. I shall make sure cook caters for them," smiled Laurent.

After dinner over cognac in the drawing room, Laurent explained who the people were in the paintings adorning the wall. All the way back to 1415 to the first Comte de Mongaudon. "After the battle of Agincourt, Charles VI 'ad been forced to accept the English 'Enry V's son as 'eir to the French throne. Charles charged six of 'is surviving knights with protecting the real 'eirs to the French throne and in return for that service made them counts along with the gift of land and wealth. Over the centuries, the succession lines of five of the six counts 'ave died out. I am the only remaining direct descendant that can trace 'is ancestry back to that time."

"Really?" said Sophia. She had no interest in medieval history but a lot in this lineage.

"Really," said Laurent with a grin realising that French history and wars were not high on Sophia's topics of discussion.

"Come on now Laurent," said Sophia. "I want some answers, please. How come you were working on a fishing boat when you have all this?"

He smiled. "I was an only lonely child. In return for the old man teaching me about the sea and fishing, when I was so alone I 'elp 'im. He refuses to take money so I give 'im five days a year of my time."

54

"You wouldn't happen to be a saint as well as a count would you?" said a very deeply impressed Sophia.

Laurent shrugged with embarrassment. "I may be many things but a saint is not one of them. So what do think of my little place 'ere then?"

"Beautiful."

"I was born 'ere. So were most of my ancestors. It means a lot to me, the 'istory and the thoughts of those who went before me."

"I was born in a barn!"

"Really? Like Jesus?"

"That's right. My parents were on holiday in Northumberland. Unfortunately, I arrived three weeks early. Dad's car broke down and Mum's waters broke. Thank goodness a passing police car stopped. A policewoman and Dad carried Mum into a barn and the nice police lady delivered me!"

"Northumberland? Where's that?" Laurent and British geography were relative strangers.

"In the north-east of England. You've heard of Newcastle United football team?"

"No, I'm a rugby man."

"I'll show you sometime on a map."

He took her by the hand and led her to the great hall. With his strong arm around her shoulder, he steered her up the magnificent staircase. At the top, he guided her left along a corridor and stopped at an oak door which he gently pushed open to reveal the master bedroom in all its glory.

A four-poster canopied bed dominated the room hung with tapestries. Sophia stepped towards the bed, turned to face Laurent and gently slipped the evening gown from her shoulders but then had to give it several tugs before it finally went over her hips to fall at her feet.

She stood there in her underwear before him. She could see the hunger for her in his eyes. And deep down inside she felt her desire for him. Slowly he raised his right hand and brushed her left breast, so gentle, so exquisite and so natural.

Laurent took hold of Sophia's hand and led her to the bed. His hand deftly unclipped her bra and he slipped it from her shoulders.

A discreet knock at the door halted progress for a moment. Bertrand through the door intoned, "Monsieur le Comte?"

"Merde." Laurent made his way to the door. "What is it?"

CHAPTER SIX

Laurent stormed out of the bedroom and slammed the door behind him leaving a bemused Sophia standing by the bed in only her knickers. She could hear his raised voice and the low tones of Bertrand but couldn't make out what was said. Laurent strode back into the bedroom. He wasn't happy.

"I'm very sorry, I 'ave to go out."

"Where? At this time of the night!"

"Come with me." It sounded more like an order than a request.

So much so Sophia was about to refuse when she decided that whatever was going on she'd better be there to find out what it was.

"Put some warm clothes on and a good pair of shoes." He ushered her out of his bedroom after draping the evening dress over her.

Laurent waited at the front of the house in a battered twenty-year-old Land Rover. He'd changed into a lumberjack shirt, jeans and boots.

Sophia appeared in a pair of jeans and jumper. The best she could find for her feet were a pair of trainers. She jumped into the scruffy car and off roared Laurent.

"Where are we going?"

"To a village not far from 'ere."

"Why?"

"Trouble I need to sort out."

"You're not armed are you?"

"No."

They both laughed. At least he'd calmed down much to her relief.

"Thought you'd have the latest four-by-four, not this old heap?" Sophia picked at the tatty upholstery.

"Never waste money on material things is my motto,"

"Says a man who lives in a chateau with servants."

Laurent threw the Land Rover along the country roads until they arrived at a picturesque little village by a small harbour. Out to sea, she could see searchlights scanning the waves.

A huddle of women gathered by the harbour. Laurent leapt from the driver's seat after skidding to a stop inches from the edge. "Wait 'ere," he commanded.

Through the window, Sophia watched Laurent in animated conversation with the women. She couldn't make out what was going on, they gabbled so quickly. Then she watched as Laurent raised his hand and the women fell silent. He spoke into his mobile phone.

Whatever he's saying, thought Sophia, he's making an issue of it. Laurent stuck the phone back in his pocket and the women went off into their animated gabbling again until Laurent merely raised his hand again and they quietened, clearly waiting for something.

Laurent yanked open the driver's door of the Land Rover.

She looked at his worried face. "What the hell is going on?" Sophia had become more than a little alarmed.

"Two fishermen failed to return tonight. All the other fishermen are out searching. The coastguard said they would wait for the morning before mounting a coordinated search. I've persuaded them otherwise." A huge grin spread across his face.

Suddenly the door beside her opened. A woman in a housecoat and boots with a scarf covering her hair eyed her up and down from a face that had lingered too long in the sun. She waved her arms. Sophia understood she was being told to get out and go with her. She looked at Laurent, he nodded his head. She climbed out and the woman led her to a white stone cottage a few yards along a narrow alley near the harbour.

Her escort lifted the latch and gently pushed Sophia inside. The room smelt a little of damp and a lot of fish. A single bulb hung from a wire in the roof. Other women from the harbour piled into the cottage behind her. A pair of hands coaxed her to a chair by a pine table. On a black range, Sophia saw and took in the aroma of what appeared to be some sort of fish soup. The woman in the housecoat tended the huge pan.

Chairs were moved, lifted and slotted in around the pine table. A young woman, about the same age as Sophia but looking worn out, passed around an assortment of bowls and spoons. The Cook carried the soup pan to the table and plonked it in the centre. While the other women helped themselves the young woman took Sophia's bowl and filled it. Bread appeared on the table and everyone tucked in.

Sophia had eaten already, but she still felt a little hungry due to leaving much of what had been on offer at the chateau. The curtailed passion had left an empty feeling in her stomach too. After a spoonful of the soup with big bits of unidentified fish floating around in it, Sophia got busy devouring the rest. It tasted delicious.

Still the women talked so fast she had trouble understanding but she managed to pick up enough to identify two women sitting at the far end of the table, not eating. They looked worried. They were the wives of the men missing at sea.

Crump, crump, crump. Sophia heard the distinct sound of a helicopter overhead heading seawards. The two women suddenly jumped to their feet and ran to the door, threw it open and dashed out to the street.

Suddenly all the other women stopped eating, put down their spoons, bowed their heads and prayed. Sophia hadn't prayed for years. Embarrassed she closed her eyes and put her hands together.

The two wives rushed back in. Through the animated conversation, Sophia managed to grasp the coastguard were out as were the navy. All eyes looked at Sophia as if she had something to do with this good news. Then she realised she was Laurent's representative. He was out there somewhere getting things done and she was basking in reflected praise. This made her even more embarrassed. It also made her realise that this man who could be so gentle could also pressure the coastguard and navy into mounting a search at night. No doubt about it, she knew, she was falling in love, not lust. Although, she mused, a little passion wouldn't be unwelcome if we ever get the chance!

Sophia watched two hours tick by. Some of the women fell asleep in their chairs but not the wives of the missing. They were up and down, in and out of the cottage all the time. Sophia followed on a couple of occasions just to get some fresh air after the stuffy room the women were using as a base.

Sophia's mobile buzzed in her pocket. She lifted it out. Laurent's number came up on the display. A flick of the green button and she heard, "Allo." Sophia listened intently to instructions from Laurent then pressed the red phone button with a deep sigh.

Sophia made her way to the centre of the room. This was going to be difficult. She'd given public talks often but telling this group of women in their language what she needed to say and get right first time outdid anything she'd done before.

Composing herself and calling on her best French she called the women over making sure the two wives were at the front and supported by their friends.

And she said what she'd been told to say by Laurent. The joy on the wives' faces, Sophia would never forget. She told them their husbands were safe and well on their way to hospital for a check-up after being found clinging to the wreckage of their boat far out at sea.

During the drive back to the chateau as the sun climbed above the horizon Laurent explained what had happened. "It seems the net got caught in something big that dragged the boat under before they had a chance to call for help."

"A rock or something, a whale?"

"No," said Laurent. We'll never know for sure but probably they hooked a submarine."

"At least it was a happy ending. I spoke to a gendarme on the quay. He said the men couldn't have lasted through the night. If you hadn't got the coastguard out they would have died." Sophia's expression relayed her profound respect for this gallant man.

"All's well that ends well."

Sophia's heart felt near to bursting with love.

CHAPTER SEVEN

Separate bedrooms and sleep revived Sophia in time for lunch. As she strolled across the sunny terrace to the table set by Bertrand, her eyes searched for Laurent but he was nowhere to be seen. The sun stood at its zenith. Crickets out in the garden clicked their happy tunes. She loosened the top two buttons on her white blouse and eased it out of the short white skirt that she'd put on in the hope of having a game of tennis. She'd spotted the court from her bedroom window.

She wandered back into the house and found the stairs that led down to the basement kitchen. Muffled voices drifted up from below. She tiptoed down each of the ancient wooden steps until she arrived at a stone flagged floor and a small corridor. Sophia listened intently. The voices came from somewhere beyond an open door through which she could see the stainless steel of an industrial sized kitchen. On she tiptoed and poked her head around the door.

The sight took her by surprise. Laurent looked so funny in a polo shirt, jeans and an apron. Bertrand held in his hands two plates on each of which Laurent placed a sea bass. He spotted Sophia.

"Cook's day off?"

"Okay, my secret's out. I'm the chef."

Bertrand led the way, inscrutable, up the stairs to the terrace where he placed the plates on the table and discreetly disappeared.

They took their seats. A little shade from a eucalyptus tree kept the afternoon sun from them. Sophia gazed out across the landscape, but she wasn't looking at the view; no she mulled over in her mind a few things that were beginning to worry her. She turned to Laurent. "Why the secrecy? Why didn't you want me to know you were doing the cooking?"

He smiled that affable smile that hit the spot for Sophia. "Not really a secret. I didn't want you to know that I was doing the cooking because I feared you may 'ave insisted on taking over. I wanted you to be 'ere and not 'ave to do any work." He took her hand in his. His soft lips brushed her fingertips.

Good answer thought Sophia, but she still wanted more. "Without being personal, in a place like this I would have thought you'd employ a cook to do the daily chores." The tingle that ran from her fingertips straight through her body from the feel of his lips on her hand made her blush.

"No. I'm trying to economise. I told you I don't like material things."

Oops! I've caused him embarrassment thought Sophia and came back with, "Oh! Sorry, I didn't want to pry. Your financial situation isn't any of my business." Why, she wondered, do I always have to put my foot in it?

"Don't worry, I'm not about to go broke. No. I 'ad a cook, Mrs Levesque, she retired last year. I thought why am I paying someone to cook for me when I'm capable of doing it myself? So I give what I would 'ave paid a cook to the 'omeless charity in town."

"You are a saint!"

Laurent's affable demeanour suddenly changed for the worse. He let go of her hand. "I told you, I'm not a saint."

"Sorry," was all she managed to come back with. It wasn't an apology though. Quite the contrary in its delivery. The perfectly cooked sea bass didn't taste at all good now. Sophia left most of it.

At last Laurent took hold of her hand again, she didn't resist. "Sophia, I'm so sorry. Forgive me. I didn't mean to upset you. It's just that, well I'm not the man you think I am."

"Don't speak to me like that again," said Sophia so forcefully that Laurent jumped with astonishment. "I'll forgive you this time. But let's make one thing clear. I do not respond to being spoken to in that manner," she heard herself say with a wince when she remembered how many times *she'd* spoken to people like that.

"You 'aven't had time for a tour of the chateau yet." Laurent hoped the sudden change of subject would help dig him out.

Sophia kissed his cheek just to show that she wasn't really cross with him. He grabbed her by the shoulders, pulled her to him and gave her a long passionate kiss on the lips just to show that he wasn't cross either. They both laughed.

Laurent proudly showed off his kitchen, all stainless steel and a massive sink you could almost have a bath in. He knew that over the centuries it must have changed many times. Great feasts would have been prepared by an army of servants. Now he did it all himself, well with the help of Bertrand. A thought flashed through his mind about what he would do in six months when Bertrand retired, but he quickly dispelled the worry. He felt it a little ostentatious to have a servant in these difficult economic times. Perhaps his future wife would insist on a cook and a butler. We'll see, he mused.

Laurent slipped the catch on the pantry door and gently pulled it open to reveal an array of hanging hams, dried sausages and a host of bottles, jars and packets. At the far end of this vast room with its wonderfully scented aromas stood an upright empty freezer with the door open. Laurent lifted a jar from a wooden shelf on the grey wall, unscrewed the lid, dipped in his finger and held it to Sophia's mouth.

"What is it?"

"It's all right. No animals have been harmed to make this fig chutney."

"You're making fun of me." She let his finger enter her mouth. She sucked the chutney off and swallowed with an unsuccessful look of submission.

It didn't fool Laurent for one second. One thing he'd discovered from this woman already was that she wasn't submissive. He took a deep breath as he withdrew his finger and hoped she didn't know what he'd just imagined.

His arm circled Sophia's back while his other hand stroked her cheek. Their lips met. He could still taste the chutney on her tongue. Gently at first he pulled her body towards him. Her firm breasts pressed into his chest. He pushed his body hard against hers and felt her quiver in his embrace. The kiss grew more impatient. He could sense that she wanted him and he knew how much he wanted her. With his powerful arms, he lifted her on to a thick pine table in the middle of the pantry knocking over jars and bottles. Quickly he undid the rest of the buttons on her blouse.

A door banged somewhere in the distance. Laurent heard heavy footsteps on the wooden stairs followed by other footsteps, less heavy. He saw that Sophia had heard them too. She buttoned her blouse just as Bertrand appeared in the doorway with a man in blue overalls carrying a metal toolbox.

"Merde," said Laurent. "I forgot the engineer was coming to repair the freezer."

On the ground floor, Laurent took Sophia on a quick tour of the drawing room and dining room before coming to a wooden door. He pushed it open, took Sophia by the hand and led her in.

A man's study says a lot about the owner thought Laurent and he felt comfortable with any interpretation that could stick to him from looking at his study. He ran his hand over a mahogany desk and its green leather insert for a writing surface. To the side of this desk stood a computer console with a flat screen and keyboard. "Please use this any time." Laurent hoped that she could do whatever she needed to do from there and so stay with him much longer. As he watched her examine the mahogany desk and the pictures on the wall, he knew how much he'd fallen for this lovely Englishwoman with the red hair.

"The real thing. Around eighteen seventy." Sophia pulled at one of the desk's drawers.

"Exactly. You know your antiques."

"Have to. It's part of my business." She moved on to examine a Japanese vase on a pedestal.

"Can you spot fakes easily?"

"Some fakes are more difficult to expose than others. Take this one." She lifted the vase. "It's supposed to be seventeenth century but look at it closely and you can see that it is not quite right. It's the right height, shape and pattern, but it isn't genuine. You can feel that by intuition sometimes."

"I paid a lot of money for that. Ten pounds in your Portobello Road a few years ago."

"If something isn't for real it usually gets found out."

Laurent decided they'd better move on quickly.

She'd seen two of the bedrooms on the next floor up so he took her into a third. Dust sheets covered everything. "I don't use this room so it's mothballed."

"I hope that isn't because it's haunted."

"What?" Laurent looked grave.

"What? I, I was joking. Don't tell me it *is* haunted!"

"About a 'undred years ago a woman was murdered in 'ere, chopped up and buried in the grounds. A dog discovered the body parts a few years later," offered Laurent. "Oh, I do 'ope that doesn't worry you. You don't believe in ghosts do you?"

"Er, not sure on that one." Sophia saw a smile creasing the side of Laurent's mouth.

Unable to keep it in any longer Laurent let out a belly laugh.

"You, you…" was all she could say. And they both laughed. It was so good to have fun again thought Sophia even if his sense of humour was a little macabre.

Laurent took Sophia to the fourth bedroom. It was the only locked room. He reached into his pocket and pulled out a small bunch of keys. Leafing through the keys he found the one he wanted and unlocked the door. Sophia saw a huge four-poster bed, tapestries on the walls and wood panelling. The windows looked out over the gardens. Her squeal of delight at a beautiful fireplace carved with cherubs and clouds made Laurent smile. She ran her hand over the cherubs. He tensed.

He toyed with the idea of showing her a secret passage behind the fireplace and decided against it. She'd just get more curious and want to have a look and then there would be more explanations. No, he wouldn't show her and he'd better keep the bedroom door locked just in case.

A flight of rickety stairs at the end of the corridor took them to the top floor. Laurent led her into the one vast room that was the attic. A row of five windows down each side gave a light, airy feel. One set looked out at the gardens and the other along the drive towards the main gates. Laurent never liked the musty smell from the many boxes stored in the attic. He always thought that if the boxes were never opened what's the point of keeping them? But he did keep them, just in case.

He gently took Sophia's arm and moved her to a window overlooking a magnificent view of the gardens.

A trip to the tenant farms and vineyards would complete the tour nicely. Laurent helped her into the old Land Rover and off they went in the warm sunshine past fields of yellow sunflowers. Lavender filled the air as they passed a lovely stone house nestling in a valley with blue lavender fields all around.

Laurent stopped at a rose surrounded gate as a happy young couple with two small children waved to them from the garden. Invited inside for a glass of wine Sophia marvelled at how well the tenants looked on Laurent. He was more than a landlord to them. She laughed as he played with the children on the floor carrying them on his back like a horse. She thought he'd make a great Dad.

In the next valley, they met an old man and his wife tending vines. Another glass of wine. Laurent explained that all the farms and vineyards were occupied by families who had lived there for generations. His aim was to continue to support this rural life for as long as he could. Perhaps it wasn't the most business like way to run the estate but he made it clear to her that people meant so much more to him than money.

"How many tenants do you have?"

"Thirty. Some 'ave vineyards and some arable and a couple rear beef. As long as I am Comte de Mongaudon they will 'ave the security of their 'omes and work."

"What would happen if you lost the estate or died without an heir?"

"The state would take it all and sell it off. The tenants would be evicted and the whole land would be a commercial enterprise without any consideration for the people who live 'ere. That's why I feel so strongly about my role in life."

Sophia couldn't help feeling the deep love for this wonderful man just keep growing inside her. And the dream of bearing him an heir flitted through her head.

On the way back to the chateau, she spotted an old church. "Is the church used?"

Laurent looked sad. "During the revolution the mob sacked it. It 'as never been reconsecrated. It is in good repair though. When a Comte de Mongaudon marries, there is always a blessing in the church.

"Can we go in?"

Laurent pulled the Land Rover into the church grounds. Sophia saw a number of well-kept graves. He saw her looking. "The churchyard is looked after by one of the farmers. Nobody is buried 'ere these days, but we respect those who were in the past."

Sophia pulled the heavy church door open and stepped in. She liked the simplicity. No garish statues or stained glass. Just solid stone walls and floor with a marble altar. She imagined standing at the altar with Laurent for a blessing on their wedding day. Would he propose to her? Was it too early? Would she accept if he did? All these questions buzzed through her mind.

He took her hand and led her back to the Land Rover.

Soon they were back at the chateau and Laurent guided her around the garden.

In the garden, Sophia was in her element. She loved gardens and had even taken a course at the Royal Horticultural Society. Daddy hadn't paid for this one. She had. And she'd picked up a lot of knowledge in a short time. One thing Sophia prided herself on was her capacity to see and remember which helped when she designed her own tiny garden on her balcony back home. Now it's probably overgrown with weeds, she thought. Gardening or lying in this man's arms, no-brainer Sophia mused.

She bent to take in the scent of a rose. As she raised her eyes, she looked at the chateau shimmering in the sunlight reflected from a small lake. How beautiful, she thought. Then she noticed something. There were seven windows on the attic floor facing the gardens. She remembered there were only five in the attic room.

CHAPTER EIGHT

Sophia insisted on cooking dinner that night. Bertrand had the night off. Laurent had strict orders that he wasn't allowed in the kitchen until called. Unusually for Sophia she'd dithered over whether to serve dinner in the dining room in all its fancy glory or have an intimate meal in the kitchen at the pine table. She'd settled on the kitchen with the hope that tonight they may actually get to make love, preferably in the bedroom rather than the pantry. But, what the hell thought Sophia, anywhere will do!

And, of course, she was an exceptional cook. Daddy had paid for the Cordon Bleu week in Paris.

A few butterflies took off in her tummy when she opened the pantry door and looked at the table in the centre where what she had dreamt of for days nearly happened.

A forage around the stores soon equipped her with everything she needed. In fact, Laurent had risen even further in her estimation with his grasp of what was required in a store cupboard. He'd even stocked the now-repaired freezer.

She wasn't sure about Bertrand. Was he trying to make a point? She'd asked him to get a chicken for her in the town when he was shopping that afternoon. And he had. Only this one came with feathers on and guts in. Sophia took it in her stride and soon had the bird plucked, drawn and oven ready.

After a couple of attempts, one nearly resulting in the loss of her eyebrows and hair, she lit the gas oven and slipped in the chicken. She didn't think Laurent would appreciate nouvelle cuisine so she'd gone for big hearty food and prepared roast potatoes, carrots, parsnips and peas to be followed by a tart tatin and a prawn salad for starters.

Her knowledge of wine was reasonable, but she'd told Laurent what he was having for his dinner and asked him to select the wine from his vast wine cellar.

At last she was ready as far as the dinner was concerned. Now she just had to get herself ready. She climbed the stairs to her bedroom and eased the little black dress from the wardrobe. The makeup took a few minutes and soon she was happy with how she looked in the full-length mirror. The dress hitched just high enough to be interesting gave her the confidence that Laurent would find her alluring.

She found him sitting on the terrace with a sketch pad and pencil. "Wow!" he exclaimed jumping to his feet as he closed the pad.

"May I see?"

Reluctantly he opened the pad. Sophia saw that he'd drawn the chateau. The perfect scale impressed her. Precision was something that she was well used to. For many of the fine items of reproduction furniture that her company made she'd done the specifications.

Sophia smiled as she watched Laurent devour his dinner. She knew there was no better compliment than an empty plate.

As she served the dessert, a few reflections ran through her brain. He's secretive. First he didn't tell me he was a count. I thought he was a poor fisherman. Then he frightens me half to death by not telling me beforehand that his 'robbery' at gunpoint wasn't for real. He didn't tell me he was the cook. What's going on with the five windows inside and seven windows outside the attic? Is he some Rochester character with a mad wife locked away up there? Why? So she said, "You play things pretty close to your chest."

"Meaning?" he replied between mouthfuls of tart tatin.

"You don't tell me things. I have to work them out. You're secretive and to be honest I'm not sure that I like that." Sophia had an edge in her voice but tried hard to make her question sound reasonable.

"I suppose you are right. I've never been very forthcoming about myself. Perhaps it's a flaw or a safety blanket. I don't know."

Sophia decided to go for broke, "What's hidden up in the attic?"

Startled, Lauren put down his spoon, "In the attic?"

"Yes, in the attic. There's a secret room up there I think. What have you got hidden? A mad wife?" She regretted this as soon as she said it. Too melodramatic and frankly bizarre.

Laurent put his hands together on the red-checked tablecloth and took a deep breath. He looked into Sophia's eyes. What was he thinking, she worried. Had she gone too far? Had she blown it? She looked back into his eyes and saw there a gentle man. A man who wouldn't harm her. A man she'd fallen in love with. She felt silly for raising the subject in such a stupid way.

"I'll show you." He took her hand and led her up the wooden stairs and then up the ornate staircase to the bedroom level. The black dress made it difficult. She

79

hitched it higher to keep up with him. Wearing the stockings may not have been such a good idea as a little white flesh peeked out from the gap between dress and stockings. Still holding her hand he guided her to the fourth bedroom door and unlocked it. She knew he'd seen the stocking tops. It gave her a thrill.

Sophia felt safe but very curious in the room. He padded across the cherry wood floor and grabbed hold of a cherub's head on the fireplace side. The whole panel opened to reveal a stone staircase leading up and down.

Without saying a word, he led Sophia by the elbow to the steps and guided her upwards. At the top of the stairs, a panelled door blocked progress. Laurent gave it a gentle push. It opened.

He went through first, reached to his left and the room filled with light from neon strips across the ceiling.

Sophia stepped in. No mad wife. No Sweeny Todd barber's shop. She saw two long tables in the centre of the room. Each table held a scale model of a building. The walls had photographs of buildings and a huge plan lay on a draftsman's board.

Laurent still didn't say anything, he just gestured to her to walk around and look. She did. The first scale model seemed to be a vast complex. Sophia had no idea what it was but by the size she reckoned it could be a new university or government offices. The second model looked like a futuristic house.

She wandered around the room looking at the photographs of modern, stylish buildings in all shapes and sizes standing in deserts, rainforests and urban areas.

A newspaper cutting pinned to the wall drew her attention. She read it in total silence. And then she turned to Laurent, "How awful!" she said feeling the words inadequate.

"Yes."

"It wasn't your fault. It says so here."

"Thirty-six people died because a building I designed collapsed, 'ow could that not be my fault?"

"It says the construction company cut corners and didn't follow your instructions."

"I was working on another project when I should 'ave kept a closer eye on the building. Yes, I was cleared of any blame but I blame myself," he said sitting down on a stool, slowly like he still had the grief within him. She put her arms around his shoulders and held him close to her.

"But why keep all this secret, hidden away up here?"

"The secret passage was already 'ere. I think 'Enri Quatre 'ad it installed during 'is religious wars in the seventeenth century. There's a lot of commercial espionage in the architectural business. I decided to use this place to make it more difficult for anyone nosing around to gain access. No mad wife I'm afraid." He managed a laugh.

"Are you working on any projects now?"

He took a deep breath. "No. I won't work as an architect again. I couldn't bear the responsibility."

Sophia kissed him lightly on the lips. Gently she pulled him to his feet and led him from the room, down the steps, through the bedroom and into the corridor.

Taking his hand in hers, she took him along the corridor to his bedroom door. A little push and the door swung open.

The late evening sun bathed the room in a sepia glow as Sophia guided Laurent towards the canopied bed with its patchwork quilt, cream silk sheets and pillowcases. Tenderly she let go of his hand and rolled back the covers. Slowly she eased the zip down the back of her dress then turned for him to continue.

His beautiful hands, hands that could pull nets into a boat and yet draw such precise plans, pulled the zip down to the small of her back. With a little wriggle, she shed the dress to stand before him in her bra, pants and stockings.

She stopped, cupped her hand to her ear.

"What?" said an almost breathless Laurent.

"Nothing. Nothing at all. Nobody to stop us now." And as the light turned to night Sophia's dreams came true in the arms of her lover.

CHAPTER NINE

Sophia awoke entwined in the strong arms of Laurent. She lay there watching the rise and fall of his hairy chest and felt a deep love developing for this wonderful man. One of his eyes opened.

He smiled. "What?"

"Just looking."

Laurent listened as the dawn brought its chorus of birds that he'd never really heard before. He gazed at the red hair as it spilt over the silk sheets. At last, he said to himself, at last I've found the woman I want to spend the rest of my life with. And then he remembered his problem. But that problem was for the future. Today and for the next few days he would enjoy being with her.

Over a breakfast of croissants and coffee Laurent said, "I 'ave an invitation to what you English would call a 'posh dinner' tomorrow night. I accepted it months ago, but I didn't want to go alone because it is for two. What do you think, would you like to go?

"I'd love to!"

"We'll take the train this afternoon." How he was looking forward to having this woman on his arm at such an event.

"The train? Why? Where are we going?"

"Paris!"

"Paris!" And she threw her arms around him hugging him close to her chest. "What should I wear?"

"We are going to be in Paris. Where else could you find anything better?"

Sophia found her passport as Laurent had asked and he disappeared into the study with it. He came out again a few minutes later.

"What was all that about?"

"Security clearance for tomorrow," he said striding off before she could ask any more questions. A little smirk crossed his mouth. Would she be impressed tomorrow night! And the day after!

They sat in a first class compartment on the TGV as it thundered north. Laurent felt very pleased with himself. He stole a glance at Sophia every few minutes to watch her engrossed in her novel. Too happy to read, he gazed out of the window at the countryside as it flashed by.

Laurent's memory of the hotel from when he was there ten years ago was still good. He'd stayed there during his first project as the architect of a complex under construction in the city. The grand foyer with a fountain surrounded by a marble floor, the massive chandelier hanging from dark stained wooden beams and that cosy smell of leather armchairs and coffee could have been held in a time warp. Much water has gone through the fountain since then, he thought.

A porter showed them to their red and white furnished bedroom. Once alone, Laurent took Sophia in his arms, "Tomorrow we go shopping. Tonight I'll find a nice little restaurant nearby."

"Can't we just have room service?" Her wicked smile didn't go unnoticed by Laurent.

They were up, showered and ready for the shopping expedition early the next day after a breakfast of chocolate and croissants under the glass ceiling of the dining room.

Somewhere nearby, a church clock chimed ten o'clock as they entered the first dress shop. Laurent had lost count of the number of shops they'd been in when he heard a clock strike midday. Still she hadn't found what she was looking for. All she knew was that it was a *very* posh do. Laurent wouldn't tell her anything further so she would keep looking until she found exactly what she was looking for.

When Laurent signalled a cab, he glanced at his wristwatch, half past two. Sophia finally had her precious dress in a pink carrier bag and a huge smile on her face.

"Why are you calling a cab?"

"To get back to the 'otel."

"Oh not yet. Got to get the shoes!"

At five fifteen a relieved Laurent put the hotel bedroom access card in the door. He kicked off his shoes and lay on the bed with throbbing feet. For a woman who says she hates shopping, he mused to himself, I'd hate to think what it would have been like if she loved shopping.

Sophia unpacked her dress and shoes oblivious to the fact that she'd worn this hunk of a man out with a simple shopping trip.

At the appointed time the bedroom phone rang, "Allo," said Laurent. "Thank you" He turned to Sophia and his heart skipped a beat. In her powder-blue silk dress and blue shoes, her red hair beautifully coiffed by the hotel hairdresser and her makeup like a film star he was nearly lost for words but just managed, "You look stunning."

She feigned a curtsey and smiled.

Her glide through the hotel foyer with Laurent in black tie drew admiring glances from all who had the pleasure to see them. The doorman opened the glass doors as they approached. Once outside, Sophia saw a black limousine with a chauffeur holding the car door open for her.

She slipped elegantly into the back seat. The driver eased the door shut with a little but expensive sounding thud. Laurent made his way round the far side and climbed in next to her. Sophia's interest in where she was going was beginning to reach a peak. She slipped her hand through the crook of Laurent's elbow and kissed him on the cheek.

"Oops," she said, wiping off the lipstick transfer.

Sophia had expected a 'posh do'. And so it was. They made their way to security. A metal detector pinged. Sophia had to turn out her clutch bag to show the offending item, her phone. Then they were free to enter an enormous ballroom with tables for ten set with silver and white linen at one end, the other end held an orchestra and a dance floor spread out between.

Already groups had gathered around the dance floor sipping champagne and nibbling canapés.

"There's someone I would like you to meet," said Laurent taking Sophia by the hand. He steered her over to a man and a blond woman standing by the far wall with their back to them. As they approached, the two turned towards them.

"Laurent, so glad you came," gushed the woman ostentatiously kissing him twice on each cheek and wrapping her very shapely body around his. Sophia saw the label on the back of her stylish long yellow dress. She knew that dressmaker charged thousands for his work. And she'd seen the face on the cover of several glossy magazines.

When Laurent disentangled himself, he reluctantly shook hands with the man. "Sophia, I would like you to meet my cousin, a distant cousin," he laughed. "Pascale and her friend Michel."

Michel was about fifty, a good twenty-five years older than Pascale in Sophia's view.

So this is *the* Pascale, said Sophia to herself, "Pleased to meet you," she offered politely to them.

"I do like your dress," purred Pascale.

Perhaps she's okay after all, mused Sophia.

"Of course yellow is *the* in colour this year," added Pascale and turned away from Sophia to engage Laurent with her deep brown eyes.

Michel smiled at Sophia, "We're all on that table over there." He pointed at a table with a number twelve flagged in the centre. "Can I get you some champagne?" Sophia noted his English was hardly accented.

Sophia nodded, a little miffed at Laurent taking so much notice of Pascale. They were talking fast in French, so fast that Sophia could hardly understand them. Michel returned with her glass of champagne.

"Your English is excellent."

"Thank you. I spend a lot of time there on business."

"What kind of business are you in?"

"Import, export," he said uncomfortably.

"What do you import, export?" she asked not really interested but trying to keep up a conversation.

"Are you trying to be funny?" said Michel suddenly stripped of his charm. He eased over to Pascale and put her and Laurent between him and Sophia.

"This is going to be a great evening I don't think," uttered Sophia under her breath.

Suddenly everybody went quiet. Sophia turned to see the French president walk into the room with his glamorous wife on his arm. The assembled throng burst into applause.

The president and his lady took their seats at table one. Everyone else made their way to their own. The other three couples at table twelve were quickly introduced. Sophia couldn't catch any of their names, but they seemed nice. Much nicer than Pascale and Michel.

Laurent leant over to Sophia and whispered, "You see that woman there on table two, the one with the jet-black hair and yellow top?"

Sophia scanned the tables until she found table two, "Yes."

"That's the president's mistress."

Sophia read the gossip magazines. She knew the president had a mistress, but she didn't expect that she would be at an official function like this. "But his wife must know. How is she going to feel about her rival being here?"

"Rival? Oh no Sophia. She's not a rival. It's just a very French arrangement." And as soon as he said it he wished he could take it back. Sophia gave him a puzzled stare and then started on her salmon mousse.

She looked up to see Michel glare in her direction and Pascale seemed to be studying her. "So what do you think of Chateau Mongaudon?" said Pascale pleasantly.

"Beautiful."

"I understand you have used some of my clothes that I keep there?" Again it was said pleasantly. No admonishment. No conflict.

"Yes. I do hope you don't mind," said Sophia thinking that Pascale wasn't so bad after all. They'd just got off to a bad start.

"No of course not. Please, help yourself to any of the things in the wardrobe," said Pascale with a smile.

"That's very kind of you," said Sophia warming to Pascale.

"I know a seamstress in the town who can let out any of the dresses for you." The stiletto expertly inserted.

Sophia toyed with the idea of a retort but decided against starting something in this company. She carried on with her mousse.

"Laurent tells me you are in the furniture business," continued Pascale in a reasonable tone.

"Yes," hissed Sophia bringing a ghost of a smile to Pascale's lips.

"I suppose that's why you have a carpenter's hands. I can also recommend a good manicurist in the town." Pascale dabbed her botox lips with her napkin.

Laurent in conversation over the troubles of the French national rugby team with two of the other men managed to keep himself out of this tete-a-tete by pretending to be unaware.

That's it! Sophia had had enough. "I understand you are a model?"

"That's right," said a superior Pascale.

"With or without your clothes on!" smiled Sophia without an ounce of mirth.

"Haven't you seen me on the covers of the top fashion magazines? Oh, of course not, you're not into fashion are you?"

"Actually I have seen you. Isn't it marvellous what they can do with an airbrush?"

"I do hope you enjoy yourself tonight. This is way above your league so if you have any worries please don't hesitate to ask me."

"You are so kind," said Sophia through gritted teeth after taking a long look at Pascale's stunning blond hair. "I can recommend a good hairdresser who will do your roots for you." Maybe not game set and match but it'll do for now thought Sophia.

Waiters moved in and cleared plates from the tables interrupting the ping-pong game. Laurent still argued with the two men about rugby. Michel fawned over Pascale. Two of the other women were in conversation about coiffure for dogs. The other couple chatted, but she couldn't hear what they were saying over the din in the room. Sophia felt the rising tide of resentment.

"Excuse me," said Sophia pushing the chair away from behind her and climbing to her feet.

The gentlemen stood. Sophia made her way to the powder room.

She sat in the gilded room touching up her makeup and quietly seething when the president's mistress walked in.

"Bonsoir," offered the newcomer.

"Bonsoir," said Sophia repairing her mascara.

"Ah, English?".

"Is my French so bad?" snapped Sophia.

"I'm sorry," said the mistress and sat on a stool alongside to repair her classy makeup.

"No, I'm sorry," said Sophia. "I'm just in a bit of a bad mood at the moment."

"I see you are with le Comte de Mongaudon, Laurent?"

"You know him?"

"Yes. He's a very nice man. Does a lot for charity. I saw you come in with him. You're sitting with Pascale."

"Yes, Pascale," said Sophia screwing up her face.

"She's... what is it you English say, a real cow! Enough to put anyone in a bad mood."

"I can think of several other names for her. And I'm not too keen on her creepy boyfriend."

"I don't know him. Looks a lot older than her. Not always a good idea."

At least I've found someone friendly reflected Sophia. She had to ask. "Look, this may sound incredibly rude because we don't know each other but may I ask you a personal question?"

"You want to know why I put up with being the president's mistress and as a result be the target of all that gossip and worse in the papers. It's all right. Lots of people ask."

"So why?" Sophia really wanted to understand this woman's point of view.

"It's simple. I love him." Her sadness touched Sophia.

"Ah, yes. Love! It makes us do things that in our right minds we wouldn't... oh I'm sorry... I didn't mean..."

"Don't worry, you are absolutely right. *C'est la vie!*"

Back at the table the main course had just arrived. Veal cutlets. Sophia didn't eat hers.

"Sorry, I didn't read the menu or I would 'ave ordered something different for you," said Laurent tucking into his cutlet.

"I've just been talking to the president's mistress. She's very nice. She knows you."

"Yes, we were once lovers."

Well that was straight out of the blue and honest, thought Sophia.

The evening did get better. Laurent paid attention to Sophia and Pascale got off her back. The meal over, the president took his wife to the dance floor and to a waltz they effortlessly glided around the room soon to be joined by other couples.

Cheltenham Ladies' College had prepared Sophia for just such an evening and in the arms of Laurent she danced the night away.

"Tell me, "said Sophia during a cha cha cha, "What is it that Michel imports and exports?"

"Pornography."

"Oh no! When I asked Pascale if she modelled with her clothes on…"

"It's all right. She isn't a porn star. 'He 'as 'is own stable of girls for that. Actually I think he's into trafficking women. Personally I can't stand him. 'E'll be arrested eventually I 'ope. But no Pascale isn't one of his victims."

"She's a difficult person to like."

"It would please me greatly if you could try to get on with 'er. I know she can be difficult." Laurent took Sophia's hand and led her back to the table.

The evening over Sophia and Laurent headed back to the hotel in the limousine.

Sophia slipped her hand through Laurent's arm. He put his hand on her knee. She smiled and snuggled closer. Laurent leant forward and pressed a button. A dark divider glass raised behind the chauffeur.

Their lips met. Laurent gently slid his hand up inside Sophia's dress. She gave a little sigh as she felt him reach the gap at the top of her stockings. She snatched at his cummerbund and in the privacy provided by the dark windows of the limousine they made love on the white leather seat. Twice.

As the limo pulled up outside the hotel and they had quickly rearranged their clothing through giggles, Sophia remembered, "The president's mistress said you do a lot for charity."

"I do what I can. I'll show you some of my work tomorrow."

CHAPTER TEN

Sophia awoke with Laurent's arms wrapped tight around her. She felt so safe, so happy with him.

His eyes flickered open. "What's the time?"

Sophia looked at the digital clock on a flat screen TV in the corner, "Half seven."

Laurent quickly extricated himself from the bed and threw on a hotel robe. "Flight is at six-thirty tonight in the meantime you have to go shopping again."

"Flight? Shopping?"

"Yes, we're off to West Africa. I'm going to show you what my charity work is. So you need some tropical clothes."

It took a while for this to sink in to Sophia. Then she wasn't sure whether she was thrilled at the prospect or irritated because he'd made plans without even discussing them with her. Eventually, she came down on the side of being thrilled. "All right, where do we do the shopping in Paris for tropical clothes?"

"I 'ave absolutely no idea but there must be somewhere, I'll ask at reception and they'll direct you where to go."

"Direct me? Us you mean."

"Actually I mean you. I've got a bag at Pascale's that I pick up when I'm passing through on one of my Africa trips. You'll 'ave to do your shopping on your own. Anyway, I doubt you particularly want to spend more time with Pascale."

Secretly she preferred to go shopping on her own but wasn't going to let him know that. "I suppose I'll just have to manage alone." And she definitely didn't want a run in with Pascale again so soon.

"You'll manage just fine I expect," said Laurent with confidence.

He took out a bundle of euros from his suitcase and handed them to Sophia.

"What's this?"

"For the clothes."

"Let's get one thing straight Laurent, I let you buy the dress yesterday because it seemed the right thing to do, but I don't want you buying my clothes for me. I'm perfectly capable of buying my own." It came out with a little more force than she intended.

A puzzled Laurent merely shrugged. He was used to women taking whatever they could from him. This one definitely had a different approach.

"How long are we going for?" This time she was more pleasant.

"Four days if that is all right with you?" Laurent's confidence sagged.

"Fine but I'll have to do some work soon as we get back." A kiss was needed at this stage she thought and planted a huge one on his lips.

They agreed to meet back at the hotel by two o'clock at the latest so they'd have time to get to the airport.

Sophia hit the shops running and apart from a diversion in the Belle Époque splendour of La Fayette department store she amassed her kit in record time and made it back to the hotel by half past one.

Laurent didn't get back until five to two which miffed her a little thinking about him and Pascale being together. For goodness sake, she said to herself, get rid of the jealousy before it becomes a problem.

Her doubts disappeared when she came out of the bathroom dressed for the flight in a knock out pair of tight jeans and equally tight top that showed off her shapely figure well. Laurent took one look at her and beamed a very happy smile.

On the way to the airport, Laurent suddenly froze and said, "I forgot to ask, are you up to date with all the shots you need for tropical climates?"

"What if I'm not?"

"We would 'ave to postpone." His grave face wasn't put on.

Sophia liked that. He cared. "I was in Borneo sourcing sustainable wood last year. I've had all the shots I need and suspect more than necessary."

"That's a relief. Don't want you getting something nasty. Not now that I've found you." He curled his arm around her shoulders and drew her close. For a moment the butterflies came back to Sophia's tummy.

The check-in with Royal Air Maroc at Paris Orly went without a hitch. Fortunately, Laurent had had the sense to book Sophia's ticket in the name of Rattigan so no difficulty over names there with the passport.

As they boarded the Boeing 737-800 Sophia felt a mounting excitement. Don't be silly, she told herself; you've travelled often enough before to exotic places. Her inner self replied that it may be so but she was now off on a real adventure this time in the company of an amazing man.

They took their seats in economy class. Sophia sat by the window not at all concerned that he'd gone for the cheapest seats. The stewardess went through the emergency procedure and soon they were airborne.

Looking down on France far below Sophia thought how lucky she was. She felt Laurent take her hand and turned to face him. He looked serious. Was something wrong, she wondered? A feeling of dread crept into her soul.

"There's something I have to say Sophia, I hope it won't make you angry or upset but I must tell you."

Sophia's elation and excitement about the trip now vanished in a flurry of worry. "What? What's wrong?" For a reason that escaped her she said it in a whisper.

"Sophia, I've fallen in love with you."

Sophia felt a lump in her throat and before she could stop them the tears flowed.

"I'm so sorry." Laurent had panic written all over his face. "I didn't know how you would take it but I had to tell you. I hope it hasn't spoilt our being together. I'm really sorry, forgive me."

Through the tears, Sophia blubbed, "Don't be an idiot. I'm crying out of happiness. You can't imagine how happy you've made me."

He threw his arms around her, their lips met and Sophia drifted off into ecstasy.

A woman's American accent from the seat behind declared, "Way to go!"

Sophia spent the rest of the three hour flight to their change over at Casablanca in the arms of Laurent. There wasn't enough time, only two and a half hours in the airport, to see the city before they were due to take the connecting flight to Abidjan in Ivory Coast. She did have enough time to dream that she was Ingrid Bergman and Humphrey Bogart would take her to Rick's. Unlike the ending in Casablanca, she would get her man. Or so she hoped. And she did have time to change her clothes from her hand baggage into a safari jacket and matching pants that were as baggy as her previous attire was tight.

Another four and a half hours on a Royal Air Maroc 737-800 and they landed at Abidjan in the Ivory Coast or as Laurent put it "Cote d'Ivoire'. The pilot announced the time there was 'oh one ten' which Sophia quickly assimilated as ten past one in the morning and what the hell were they going to do there at this time?

An uncomfortable night on a bench at Abidjan airport couldn't dampen Sophia's enthusiasm though. She went outside to watch the sunrise over Africa leaving

Laurent asleep on their luggage. Sophia was spellbound by the sight and sounds.

A one-hour flight on a twelve seater plane took them the hundred and forty-three miles to Sassandra at the mouth of the river of that name. The trip ran parallel to the coast and from her vantage point Sophia looked down on the clear sea below and the tiny dots that she thought were fishing boats.

Sassandra wasn't exactly romantic and she was glad when a friendly local introduced by Laurent as Jean-Michel helped them load their kit into the back of an ancient pick-up truck. She couldn't understand much of what Jean-Michel said in his patois, but she gathered he was very pleased to see Laurent and was curious about her.

A fifteen mile drive along an unmetalled road with Sophia jammed in the middle between Laurent and Jean-Michel shook off the lethargy of the flights. Through the scrub, forest and a couple of poor villages they weaved before they finally arrived at their destination. 'Mutenye' a village of traditional huts nestling on higher ground from a white beach and the gentle rolling waves of the Atlantic took Sophia by surprise by its sheer beauty.

Jean-Michel unloaded their bags and with a handshake for Laurent and a massive smile for her he disappeared off into one of the huts.

"So this is it," said Laurent. "This is where I spend my in'eritance."

Just then a whole bunch of kids, perhaps twenty-five strong, came charging towards them, laughing and shouting.

"Schools out!" Laurent laughed as the children ran round and round them like Apaches around a wagon train. Women in brightly coloured dresses came out of the huts all clearly happy to see Laurent. An old man with a shock of white hair limped out of a hut. He carried a pole as a walking stick. Laurent strode over to him and shook his hand. He seemed to be introducing Sophia so she made her way towards them. The old man took a couple of steps back as she approached.

"What's wrong?" Sophia was a little miffed in case women in this village were second-class citizens which was something that she would not support.

"He's never seen anyone with red hair before." Laurent touched her flowing locks.

The old man turned out to be the village elder. He took Sophia on a tour of the village introducing her to the women while Laurent wandered off down the beach to speak to some fishermen.

Some of the women Sophia met sat cross-legged on the ground weaving baskets with great dexterity. Everyone seemed amused at the colour of her hair. Sophia thought how friendly everyone was.

On the edge of the village, they came to the school under a thatched roof. The throng of kids that had swarmed around them when they arrived were back in class. A pretty African teacher about twenty years old in a colourful dress stood at the front of thirty children in white shirts and black shorts or black skirts sitting at desks.

The pupils craned their necks to look at Sophia. "Bonjour," said the teacher.

"Bonjour," said Sophia.

"I speak a little English," said the teacher with hardly a trace of an accent.

The children's excitement grew, but their behaviour Sophia noticed with admiration was perfect.

"We are very indebted to Laurent," said the teacher.

Laurent? She's on first name terms with him? That little demon jealousy crept into her mind again.

"Yes. He's done so much for us. He subsidises the fishing, put in the water supply built and financed this school and paid for my training."

And what did you give him in return? She thought but didn't say.

"And he's funded the clinic," said a voice behind her. She turned to see a young European woman in a nurse's white dress. "Pleased to meet you. I'm Jane Cross from Salisbury."

Seems he's into funding good-looking women, deliberated Sophia. "Hi, Sophia MacDonald from London." They shook hands. Jane led Sophia into a white hut next to the school. Inside she found three hospital beds with one occupied by an expectant mother.

"We have a doctor come by once a week but the rest of the time it is down to me I'm afraid. None of this would exist without Laurent," said Jane.

First name terms again! The green monster lurked just beneath Sophia's surface.

In a long hut open on all sides under a palm leaf roof Sophia found a pile of carved animals, elephant, lion, zebra and grotesque face masks sitting on cocoanut matting in the centre of the room. Some worn tools lay on the ground but the people who made the animals were nowhere to be seen. The elder tried hard with sign language to explain where the men were. Sophia wasn't sure if she got the message right but if she did then they were out at sea fishing and the carving was a side-line for this cooperative village.

A young woman came out of a hut with a baby on her hip and a white flower in her hand. Respectfully she gave the flower to the elder. He took it from her with a smile and gently placed it in Sophia's hair just above her right ear. She just hoped it didn't have any bugs in it.

Laurent and Sophia didn't have any time to change before they found themselves as guests of honour that night at a meal on the beach with fish cooked on a bonfire. She wasn't sure what the fish was and Laurent didn't know but it tasted so good in that place. Sophia felt so relaxed and so welcome among these friendly people who had very little but happily shared what they had with her. What a pleasant change from the backbiting and shenanigans back home, she thought. But the jealousy lingered just at the back of her mind.

And the women were not second class. In fact, she soon picked up that they were the ones who ran things. The teacher and nurse were nowhere to be seen.

Laurent finished off his fish and wiped his hands on a palm leaf. "There won't be many of these parties in the future."

"Why not?"

"Over fishing. These guys barely make a living."

"And yet they do all this for us? Well for you. I've seen what you do for this village."

A huge moon reflected in a glass-like sea, insects filled the air with their cacophony of sounds and Sophia turned to Laurent sitting on the sand with his arm around her shoulders. "I love you too."

He kissed her gently on the lips. She closed her eyes and then quickly opened them again when she heard laughter and clapping. The villagers all stared at the happy couple.

The head man with his stick led the way while a bunch of strong young men carried Laurent and Sophia on a wicker litter to a little thatched hut on the edge of the village. There they were deposited and left as the villagers melted into the night. Laurent took Sophia's hand and led her inside.

Oil lamps made from bean tins lit the inside. A bamboo bed with palm leaves for a mattress filled most of the room.

Two pairs of eyes searched each other. Laurent gently slipped off Sophia's safari jacket and hoisted her khaki shirt over her head. Slowly she unbuttoned his shirt and let it slide off his muscled torso. Tenderly she unbuckled his belt. Deftly he undid her belt. And then their passion exploded in that little hut. Even the collapsing bamboo bed couldn't dampen their fervour until at last, spent, they lay in each other's arms listening to the sounds of Africa outside their love nest.

Sophia wondered what tomorrow would bring.

CHAPTER ELEVEN

A commotion outside woke Sophia first and then Laurent. "Something's wrong," said Sophia.

Laurent threw on his clothes and peered out of the hut to see villagers running towards the beach. Sophia quickly dressed, banged her shoes on the ground to make sure no six-legged inhabitants had crept in during the night and together they set off to find out what the fuss was about.

On the beach, they saw lines of fishermen launching their boats and wildly waving to a boat far out at sea. "What is it?" asked Sophia.

"Pirate fishermen."

"What? Pirates? You're kidding me."

"No. European fishermen come for the pickings. There's a law against them taking stocks here but nobody to enforce that law. So they get away with it."

Sophia could see his anger. "What are the people going to do?"

"Try to stop them I guess. Stay 'ere." Laurent climbed into a boat being launched from the beach.

Sophia watched him head out to sea in the small flotilla. As he stood in the prow of the boat, it reminded her of that scene in 'Mutiny on the Bounty' where Marlon

Brando headed for shore to woo the chief's daughter in Tahiti. This wasn't Tahiti, but she bet that Laurent would have given Brando a good run for his money.

Sophia wasn't good at doing as ordered. She jumped aboard the last boat launched. The three villagers already inside gazed at her with surprise that quickly turned to admiration. She decided against standing in the prow like Laurent and instead sat as inconspicuous as was possible in this small open boat.

When Sophia's boat reached the pirate trawler the other villagers had it surrounded and with machetes were hacking through the nets.

Laurent was in the thick of the frenzy wielding his machete like a man possessed. On the deck of the offending boat, Sophia could see three men, one armed with a shotgun. Her stomach turned over when she saw him lift the gun and take aim at Laurent's boat.

Bang! A cloud of smoke rose over the three desperate crew. A villager beside Laurent tumbled into the water. Laurent and his crew mates pulled him back aboard and set off for the shore as fast as the little boat would go. Sophia kept her head down so he wouldn't see her. She didn't want to interfere with the need to get the wounded man to medical aid.

Incensed the villagers swarmed over the gunwales of the trawler. The three crewmen including the one with the shotgun backed up to the bow as the villagers prowled the deck towards them, machetes at the ready.

Sophia's brain went into overdrive. She leapt aboard the trawler and placed herself firmly between the opposing factions. From the frightened shouting coming from the bow, she gathered the three Europeans were Spanish. She didn't speak Spanish but made it clear to them that they were not to fire. She somehow managed to calm the villagers and get them off the trawler. And then in sign language she told Spaniards to clear off immediately.

The villagers headed for the shore triumphant about their victory and all the way back the boats converged on Sophia's to heap praise on her brave action. The trawler headed out to sea. Sophia realised what she had just done and threw up into the blue ocean to the amusement of the village men.

Laurent waited on the shore. When her boat beached, he rushed to her. "I told you to stay 'ere!" He engulfed her in his strong arms.

"How's the guy who got shot?" Happy that Laurent was so concerned about her.

"OK. Just superficial. Jane's treating 'im in the clinic." He hugged her tight.

"Something needs to be done before someone gets killed."

"I don't know what we can do. The authorities 'aven't got the resources to patrol this area. The European Union condemns the actions of the pirates, but they turn a blind eye. What can we do?"

"I don't know but we must do something. We need to make sure the villagers don't get murdered or murder anyone."

"Just like that?" said Laurent slightly put out that in his largesse she was taking over. "Do you 'ave any ideas?"

"I do have the germ of an idea."

CHAPTER TWELVE

Sophia took Laurent by the hand and led him to the long hut that held the carved pieces. "What happens to these?"

"They're sold to a dealer who ships them abroad. They sell in the shops in New York and London, not for much, the market isn't good for this sort of thing. The guys who make them get very little." Sophia sensed his puzzlement at her interest in such carvings.

"I thought so," she said picking up a beautifully made elephant. "The people who made these know about wood." Sophia marvelled at the intricate skill.

"Well yes, they do. What is it you are thinking? Cut out the middle man and market them ourselves? I don't think so. We don't 'ave the distribution network or the expertise. And the profit margin is small."

"Where do they get the wood from?"

"There's a logging station just down the coast. They beg for bits of spare timber."

Sophia didn't say anything. She just stood there thinking.

"Ah, I understand. You would like to take the pieces and sell them through your network? That's possible. Not sure that it would make much difference to what the artisans get paid though."

"No. The time and effort that goes into making these isn't reflected in the sale price." She stroked her chin deep in thought. Sophia rummaged around in a barrel of pieces of wood. "Iroko, idigbo, mahogany," she said carefully examining the offcuts. "Come on we're going to school!" And she pulled him by the hand.

Break time exploded as they reached the school with the kids piling out into the hard clay playground to use their pent-up energy. The pretty teacher wandered over to Laurent and Sophia. That little tinge of jealousy crept up when the teacher kissed Laurent on both cheeks, but she quickly subdued it and said, "Could I have some paper, a pencil and a ruler, please?"

The teacher looked at Laurent. He shrugged and nodded. "Follow me," she said in that almost perfect English.

Inside the classroom, the teacher supplied the sought articles. Sophia sat at a desk that was far too small for her and set about her task with the sound of kids doing what kids do at school playtime.

Laurent watched her with increasing interest. After five minutes, Sophia stood and showed him what she had drawn. Four mortise and tenon joints with measurements.

"What's this about?"

"The germ of an idea! The wood carvers know all about wood. I know all about making furniture. My knowledge pooled with their skill equals a project that could bring in enough work so they wouldn't have to rely on the dwindling fish stock."

He looked at her with those blue eyes, but she could see he doubted her. "Make furniture 'ere and ship it where?" He shook his head.

"Wherever there is a market to buy it." Sophia had reverted to business mode to which she was well suited.

"Reproduction Chippendale and Louis XIV chairs?"

"African and Arab will be the style!"

The logging station down the coast had another advantage. A communication aerial provided a footprint for Sophia's smartphone that allowed her to access the Internet. Her thumbs soon tapped out a query for her team back at the factory to work out. What was the weight of a one metre by half a metre by half a metre table made from iroko? She'd seen in Zanzibar a few years earlier the type of table that she was now costing. What is the cost of shipping that item by land for one hundred and forty-three miles to the airport at Abidjan? What is the cost of flying that item from Abidjan to the Arabian Gulf? And as an alternative by sea?

Now she turned her attention to the work. "Gather the men at the carving hut, please. And you'd best ask the teacher to come along as well to act as interpreter."

Laurent shrugged his Gallic shoulders. His annoyance at her taking charge had changed to one of admiration for her direct and professional approach. If anyone was going to be able to transform a backwoods carving hut into a furniture factory he was looking at her.

Sophia had expected half a dozen or so men to turn up. When she walked into the carving hut her eyes opened wide at the sight of at least thirty men and as many women crammed in to see what this woman with the strange hair was going to do now. The pretty teacher smiled at her.

Through her interpreter, Sophia showed the men and some of the women the drawing of the joints. After much laughter, two men stepped forward to be the guinea pigs.

Sophia and Laurent adjourned to the beach and sat on a log to look out at the sea.

"If this works I need to go inland to make sure the timber is from a sustainable source," said Sophia flicking a hungry insect off Laurent's neck.

"It won't be easy. But there is a reasonable road up there which they bring the logs down."

Two hours later the guinea pigs presented Sophia with four perfect mortise and tenon joints. One hour after that a text came on her phone with the costs she'd asked for. She already had a sum in mind for the retail price of the table that she would sell through her own distribution network. Sophia knew the price of timber. She lay down on her back to work out the viability of her project. "Right! We're on, subject to my approval of the logging setup," she pronounced. "The village will make enough to support itself without the fishing and have a little extra besides. I want to make sure they're not ripped off so I will personally take charge of this project."

"You'll be making more than tables then?"

"Oh yes! There's a whole range of things that these guys can make. So, when can we go upcountry for the logging?"

"Tomorrow."

"One more thing."

"What?" Laurent had just a slight hint of concern.

"You are an architect. I don't want anything fancy, but I need a large hut with a concrete floor and walls. There will be machinery and tools in the building and though I'm sure that nobody in the village would steal anything I want it all safe from passing opportunists."

"You know I don't work as an architect any longer."

"Quit whining and get it done."

Laurent opened his mouth to give her a dressing down for being so rude and then stopped, smiled and said, "OK milady!"

Sophia realised she had probably overstepped the mark. She took his hand, kissed it and then kissed his lips. "Sorry! I'm just trying to help."

"I know." Laurent rose to his feet and pulled her to hers. "A lie down before lunch?"

"Back to the hut then!"

He looked up and down the deserted beach and then over at an upturned boat on the sand. "No!" He grabbed her by the arm, lifted her over his shoulder and set off at a run towards the overturned boat. She squealed with delight. Gently he lowered her to the sand, bent down and pulled her under the boat. With lightning speed, he had her clothes off and laid her on her back on top of them.

His slow rhythm fell into pace with the soothing lapping of the waves. Sophia lay in her own private heaven.

The next day at the logging station, Sophia turned her ample charm on the logging manager, Jacques, introduced by Laurent as one of the first pupils at the village school. Sophia reckoned he couldn't be more than twenty-three, but his quiet professionalism impressed her deeply. He didn't speak English. His French was first-class without patois. She explained her quest. He was happy to show off his eco-friendly operation even taking it upon himself to drive them the fifty miles upcountry to the logging project in a battered Range Rover. The two guys in the back armed with Kalashnikovs did cause her a little anxiety until Jacques explained that bandits sometimes hijacked vehicles going to and from the logging project. After that, she was more than happy to have them behind her.

All they met on the route were two trucks loaded with timber heading in the opposite direction. After two hours of bumping along the poor road, they arrived at the logging site.

Laurent handed her down from the boneshaker as Jacques jumped out the other side. A big smile from Jacques and a wave of his hand was his invitation for

Sophia to look wherever she wanted to as he passed her a hard hat and cautioned her to take care.

Her guide, Charlotte about the same age as Jacques, in good French, explained that she was also an ex-village school pupil. Sophia could see how Laurent's input had improved the lot of the villagers so they could go forward with self-help rather than depend on international aid. The support was still needed for now to keep the school and clinic running. Sophia had no doubt the teacher was also an ex-pupil.

Charlotte guided Sophia through the complex without dictating where she could go. Laurent stayed back at the Range Rover with Jacques.

In a clearing, Sophia found lines of saplings. Charlotte explained that for every tree felled they planted four of the same species.

They watched a team of men expertly cut a huge tree so it fell between other trees without damaging them. Sophia had seen such operations all over the world, but this one was special. These guys really cared, she thought.

Back at the Range Rover Sophia thanked Charlotte for the tour and Jacques for his management of the project. She jumped in ready for the trip back to the village.

"Where are you going?" asked a puzzled Laurent.

"Back to the village, aren't we?"

"It'll be dark soon, too dangerous to travel. Jacques says we must stay 'ere tonight." He could see the lack of enthusiasm for the idea on Sophia's face. "Sorry, but it's necessary."

She'd spent the night out in tropical rainforests before, in Borneo. There was nothing romantic about it. Hot, sticky and plagued with insects were the memories etched into her mind. "So where are we sleeping?"

"Over there!" She followed his gaze to a long hut. Not exactly a hut, more a roof on poles open at the sides she thought. And then she saw the rows of camp beds.

Oh that's charming I don't think, she said to herself. Like being back at Cheltenham Ladies' College dorm except here I'm sharing with guys and nasties that'll want to eat me all night. She didn't let Laurent know her worries. After all, it had been a really successful day and she didn't want to spoil it.

The night closed in and all the workers, about fifteen of them, gathered around a campfire. Jacques and Charlotte sat together and Sophia could see clearly that they were an item.

A large animal roasted on a spit over the fire. One of the workers tended it while another handed round mugs of some alcohol that Sophia couldn't identify but after the initial stripping of her taste buds it went down all right.

Finally, the cook decided the meat had been cooked enough. He cut slices off and handed them around. Sophia got the first offering and Laurent the second. She had no idea what the animal was but hunger overtook her squeamishness about animal welfare and she couldn't taste anything anyway after the alcohol.

One of the workers produced a guitar. Charlotte sang along in a haunting melody. The alcohol, food, atmosphere and company all conspired to make Sophia look at Laurent and smile. "I love you so," she said.

He put his arm around her shoulders and drew her to him, her head on his chest. "I love you too."

She looked up when Charlotte finished singing to see her and Jacques quietly walking away into the darkness.

In the excuse for a dormitory, Sophia discovered a blanket across the room to separate two camp beds from the others. One mosquito net covered the two beds. The blanket only came up about six feet with a gap to the ceiling of about eight feet. Still, thought Sophia, there is some privacy for me to get into bed.

She wasn't too keen to undress because of the buzzing insects so she slipped fully clothed under the net. Laurent did the same.

The long day and alcohol caught up with her and soon she was fast asleep. Some animal out in the forest shrieked in the middle of the night waking Sophia. She looked over at Laurent whom she could just make out in the moonlight filtering through the side of the hut and the net.

"What the hell was that?"

"No idea."

Laurent's hand crept across the narrow gap between their beds and wandered along the side of her body.

"Not here! Someone will hear us." But to no avail, the hand worked its magic and soon he was alongside her on the narrow camp bed. "We can't," she pleaded through a giggle.

Laurent was on a mission and she had neither the will nor wish to stop him. It wasn't the most romantic assignation she had ever enjoyed. In the future when she looked back on it, the encounter would be up there as one of the funniest things she had ever done. She had no idea how they got through it with the giggles and creaking bed without waking the others.

Charlotte waved them goodbye in the morning as Jacques, Laurent and Sophia headed back to the coast. Sophia had no idea where Jacques and Charlotte had spent the night, but the body language between them at the farewell suggested that it had been mutually enjoyable.

The rough road back took two hours. Sophia couldn't stop the occasional giggle when she thought about herself and Laurent on the camp bed.

On their last night before heading back to France Sophia went through a checklist with Laurent. Everything was in place. The furniture workshop would be ready in two months by which time she would have sourced all the tools. Jacques had promised to give them a good deal on timber and to print off the technical drawings that she would send through for the villages to work from. Sophia and Laurent sat on the beach watching the huge tropical moon rise in the sky.

Laurent said, "There's another village a couple miles down the coast from 'ere that I want to 'elp. They're boat builders for the fishermen but with the fish stocks nearly gone nobody wants boats."

"Let me get the furniture project off the ground and then I'll take a look at your boat builders."

"Get them making furniture too?"

"No. If they are good and I'm sure they are, we'll go into the boat business and export what they make."

"You are unbelievable."

"Unbelievable?"

"In the nicest possible way I meant."

"No, Laurent. Whatever I say I mean. I don't like false promises or lies. And I expect other people to be the same."

It had been hectic and Sophia knew that she had sometimes been a little too forthright. As she sat there with Laurent watching the tropical moon, she sensed there was something bothering him. Something important that he wasn't telling her. She longed to ask him, interrogate him even, but she knew better than that and decided to let things take their course. If he needed to tell her something he would.

CHAPTER THIRTEEN

Bertrand collected them from the airport in the old Land Rover. The journey from Africa had been uneventful. Well apart from Sophia kneeing a security guard between the legs at Abidjan airport when his hand lingered over her breast with a feeble excuse that he was checking the pocket in her safari jacket. A rapid intervention by Laurent stopped her arrest or worse.

She had enjoyed the trip. At last there was something useful she could do. And who better to do it with than Mr Wonderful?

Laurent gave Bertrand the night off even though he'd had every night off while they had been away. Sophia cooked supper of monkfish wrapped in Parma ham and served it on a bed of couscous which they ate in the kitchen. Sophia much preferred the cosy surroundings there to the formal dining room with its generations of nobility looking down at her from their lofty perches on the walls.

Sophia noticed that Laurent drank rather more than normal. The meal over, they adjourned to the drawing room where he sipped a cognac. She settled for a coffee. Something's wrong, she worried. "Don't worry about

Africa. It'll be fine. We'll get everything sorted in a couple of months," she comforted.

Laurent rose to his feet, a little unsteady. "I have to tell you before you find out anyway."

Sophia's blood ran cold. Something *was* wrong.

"I told you about my in'eritance. I spend it 'elping the villagers in Africa and the fishermen 'ere we met the night the two went missing."

"Yes?"

"Well, I need my in'eritance to 'elp them. There's a covenant on my in'eritance."

"So?" A horrible feeling squished around her tummy.

"The covenant says that no Comte de Mongaudon is allowed to marry an English born woman. It's there because of the fear of treachery all those years ago. If I marry an English born woman I lose my 'ouse, title, lands and income. They all go to the government and the government will snap them up in the current economic state." He slugged another gulp of cognac.

Sophia couldn't hide her disappointment though she hadn't really thought about marriage other than in daydreaming. "Well, to be honest I'm not happy about that. Not that I expected you to propose to me, yet. I just don't like the idea of that stupid covenant. It's an insult. Anyway, I can live with that. Thanks for being so honest. I know it must have been troubling you." She leant forward and kissed him on the lips. "We can still work on the Africa project and spend our nights together. You're not getting away from me on that feeble excuse."

"I checked your passport. It says your place of birth is Northumberland, England. If only you'd been born in France or Italy or Spain. Anywhere but England."

"You can't choose where you are born so that's an end to it. We won't be getting married and we'll have to live in sin."

Laurent looked visibly relieved. They would get over it, she thought. She wasn't going to let him go. Not now she'd found him and loved him so.

"I'm so glad you feel that way," said Laurent. "I thought you would expect to be my wife and I would love to marry you but the circumstances dictate that it is not possible."

"Enough," said Sophia. "Let's just leave it there."

"One other thing. The question of an 'eir. I need one to carry on the family name. I've arranged to marry Pascale in two months.

It felt like a kick in the stomach. Sophia gasped.

He carried on, not looking at her. "She wants a baby because her friends all 'ave one. She wants the respectability of marriage to someone like me without the restraints of a real commitment so it works for both of us. I can carry on with you and she can carry on with her current lover or anyone she wishes once she has produced my 'eir. A very French arrangement."

CHAPTER FOURTEEN

Sophia still seethed as the plane flew over the English Channel though she couldn't see anything for the dense cloud. She wouldn't have countenanced the arrangement with anyone he decided to marry for convenience but aargh she screamed inside, Pascale!

To top it all she waited at the baggage carousel for her suitcase in vain. The police escorted her from the airport while the lost luggage clerk sneaked off for a strong drink to get over the verbal abuse she'd given him.

So it was a sullen Sophia that arrived at her Chelsea flat. She let herself in to the lonely apartment, poured a whisky, sat on the sofa and cried and cried. Night came but still she sat on the sofa sobbing her heart out. The whisky bottle didn't help.

A dull wet day greeted Sophia when she awoke with the empty bottle in her lap and a pain in the shoulder from sleeping in an awkward position. The bathroom mirror brought her up with a start. Gazing back at her was a woman with dark circles under bloodshot eyes, puffy cheeks and hair like the wreck of the Hesperus.

Her power shower pumped some life back. An empty fridge forced her to dress and make her way down to the convenience store hoping she wouldn't meet anyone she knew. She didn't. Armed with half a dozen eggs, bread and milk she scurried back to her flat. And there she stayed for three days living off her freezer contents not that she had much appetite.

By day four the eyes had returned to normal, a glow reappeared on her cheeks and a visit the hairdresser that morning repaired the damage. She knew she had to face going back to work. That afternoon would be her D-Day.

Sophia took a deep breath, smoothed down her tight black skirt, jacket and white silk blouse. She glanced up as she walked under the sign 'MacDonald Furniture Co Ltd' through the revolving glass doors and into the smart white marble and teak reception of her business.

A quick nod at the alarmed receptionist and Sophia clicked across the floor to the elevator. She strode down the second floor corridor to her office guarded by Jane, her secretary.

"We didn't expect you back so soon Ms MacDonald," said Jane lamely stuffing coffee cups and paper into drawers.

"Well, I'm back now, bring me coffee." Sophia threw her office door open stormed in and slammed it behind her.

It took just over a week for Sophia to regain her composure by which time the rest of her office staff was close to mutiny. Fortunately, she'd stayed away from the factory floor or there would have been a strike.

Sophia sat in her office gazing out on her view of London. France it was not but picturesque nevertheless if you avoided looking at some of the modern monstrous buildings. She wondered what Laurent with his architect's hat on would say about those buildings and then pinched herself as she found her thoughts wandering to the good times they had spent together.

***

Reverend Dr Phillipa Millward Ph.D. sat on a pew in the Victorian church while Sophia related her woes. "So what do you think Phillipa?"

"Sounds like quite a man to me. Look Sophia, we've known each other since uni, I know you are not the type to accept second place in this guy's life. Move on."

"But it's eating away at me," said Sophia. "What would be the church's view?"

"You know that without me telling you."

"So I have to move on?"

"If this man really loved you he would give up everything for you. But… but if you love him, then fight for him! To hell, oops, with what the church says, go for it girl!"

"But if he gave everything up for me what would all those people who depend on him do?"

"He doesn't know you're a rich woman?"

"No."

"Perhaps you could take over his charity. You've already made a big impact with your furniture project out there."

"I could but I don't think he would like that. He's not the kind of guy who would want to live off a rich wife."

Back in her office Sophia picked up the intercom, "Get me Charlie the Rat!"

"Mr Rattigan?" queried Jane.

"YES!"

Charlie Rattigan, in a pinstripe suit, white shirt and yellow silk tie slouched through the door and flashed an expensive smile at Sophia sitting behind her desk. She narrowed her eyes in reply.

"Well now Mrs Rattigan, sorry, Ms MacDonald it is now, what can be so urgent that you have me summoned to your lair?"

"You owe me a favour," spat Sophia desperately trying to keep her loathing under control.

"I suppose I do since you saved me from being disbarred. Who do you want me to kill or maim?"

"Don't be flippant. You are one of the best lawyers in this city and I need some legal advice."

"Don't sell me short Sophia. I am the best lawyer in this city and most other cities too!"

"I haven't time for this," said Sophia handing him a file. "I want you to go to the National Library in Paris and research what is in the file. I need to know whether this contract from six hundred years ago is still legal."

"What makes you think I have time to do that?"

"If you don't you'll have all the time on your hands you need when I regain my memory about you screwing a vulnerable client and you're disbarred!" she hissed.

"Blackmail!"

"You're damned right, now get on with it!"

"You are such a charmer. How could I ever have fallen out of love with you?"

The days turned into weeks. Still Charlie the Rat hadn't come up with anything concrete. All he could give her was that it didn't look good for her. Each time she berated him to come up with a definite answer he had some excuse, the last one being the need to wait for a better translation of the covenant document. Sophia's mood didn't improve much as the date for Laurent and Pascale's wedding loomed.

Sophia and Phillipa picked their way through a Chinese meal and a bottle of wine.

"I've decided," said Sophia. "I'm going back to France and I'm going to try to knock some sense into Laurent's thick head. If he won't change his mind about marrying that Pascale then I'll tell him I'm rich and can support his charity if he drops Pascale."

"Oh dear! What if he won't be a kept man?"

"Last resort, I'll be his bloody mistress. I can't live without him."

"Hmm. How's Charlie the Rat coming on with his legal investigation?"

"It's taking too long. I can't wait any longer or the marriage will go ahead before I'm able to put my case properly."

"I hope you know what you are doing Sophia."

"I don't. But I have to try."

Sophia checked her baggage in at the business class counter and made her way through security to the Gatwick departure lounge. Butterflies filled her tummy.

She tried a cup of what passed for coffee to calm them and tried to read the newspaper with one eye on the departures screen.

Her flight number and gate eventually came up. She hurried to the gate. What had been a bold and brave decision now seemed fraught with doubts. She wouldn't surrender. Fight for her man Phillipa had said. Sophia would fight.

Deep in thought she sped along the concourse. Streams of incoming passengers passed in the opposite direction on the other side of the glass partition.

Suddenly she was aware of a loud tapping noise alongside her. She looked round to see Laurent on the incoming side of the concourse tapping a key on the glass to attract her attention.

I'm dreaming, she thought. Then the realisation, it really was him. He said something. What was he saying? She couldn't hear him through the glass with all the other noise around.

A tubby woman police sergeant toting a carbine with her male colleague at her side sauntered along the concourse towards her.

Laurent mimed something. She still couldn't hear. He pulled a book and pen from his shoulder bag and turned to the inside back cover. Sophia heartbeat pounded in her ears. She watched him go down on one knee and write, *'I don't care if I lose my title and my estate. I love you. Will you marry me?'*

Desperate to contain her tears of joy she nodded her head.

"Move along there," said the constable to Sophia.

The woman sergeant looked at Laurent on his knees and read what was on the paper. "Come with me luv," she smiled taking Sophia by the arm.

"But Sarge," protested the constable.

"Oh do shut up Peter." She led Sophia through a door, down a flight of stairs, up another and out into the strong arms of Laurent.

The sergeant ushered them into a small office, closed the door and stood guard outside.

After three minutes of intense kissing they came up for air. "You're giving everything up for me?" gasped a breathless Sophia.

"Yes. I can't live without you."

"But what about Africa, the school, the clinic, the French fishermen and your tenants?"

"I'm working as an architect again. I can support my charities from what I earn. And I can support you too without my in'eritance. I'm working out a deal with the authorities to let the tenants stay on their farms for five years and then I'll 'elp them resettle."

"How did poor Pascale take it?" asked Sophia trying not to show her true feelings.

"Not well to put it mildly. 'Ow I could ever 'ave thought of living with that woman I do not know."

"I can help with the charities. I have some money."

"We'll see," said Laurent.

"No, we won't bloody see," said Sophia indignantly. "I will help and don't you even think of not letting me."

Laurent raised his hands in mock surrender. They both laughed.

"All we 'ave to do now is arrange the marriage. England or France?"

"Before they take everything away from you, can we have a blessing in the Chateau's church?

"I don't see why not," smiled Laurent enfolding her in his strong arms. Another passionate kiss ended when the sergeant banged on the door and told them they'd have to come out.

Sophia joy suddenly tempered with the thought that he'd lose the title, his lands and many people would be worse off because of her happiness. Perhaps in a few years he would blame her and regret the marriage. Perhaps... No! I want to marry him and I will, she said to herself.

CHAPTER FIFTEEN

September came and with it the cooler air just right for a wedding in the South of France. Sophia made all the arrangements for the caterer, the flowers, the wedding lunch and all those little pieces that together make up the perfect day.

Laurent had explained the procedure to her about the separation of church from state. For legal reasons the Mayor would officiate at the Town Hall for the civil part of the marriage. A blessing in the church by Sophia's friend Phillipa in her vicar's role would follow. Sophia being divorced didn't affect the church part because the church wasn't consecrated now and it would be a blessing, not a religious service.

In the whirl of events since the airport meeting Sophia found it hard to believe that only three weeks had passed. She stood in front of the mirror in her chateau bedroom and looked at the canary yellow long dress that she'd bought in Paris. Laurent's suggestion that she could wear one of Pascale's dresses had not been appreciated. Pascale hadn't replied to the wedding invitation and she hadn't collected her things from the chateau. Phillipa in her grey suit and dog collar fussed around Sophia smoothing and picking until satisfied the bride was ready.

Sophia's Mum and Dad were still bobbing about in the South Pacific. They wouldn't be able to make the wedding in person. The excellent aid of technology ensured they would be there on a screen and able to see everything too.

And so the time came. Still that niggling doubt wouldn't leave Sophia's head. Was she selfish? Would Laurent regret the marriage later? She kept all this to herself and with Phillipa made her elegant way to the sixties Citroen Safari decked out in lace and ribbons for her journey to the town hall with Bertrand as the chauffeur.

Sophia inched her mobile phone out of her tiny handbag. She passed it to Phillipa. "It's on vibrating but I don't want it going off and making me jump out of my skin." Phillipa slipped it into her grey pocket.

The French tricolour fluttered in the sea breeze from a pole on the façade of the stone built town hall. Bertrand pulled the Citroen to a gentle stop. Sophia and Phillipa climbed out to cheers from onlookers who stopped to see the lovely bride.

Inside the town hall Sophia could smell polish and quality wood as she glided to the wedding chamber with Phillipa still fussing alongside her.

Phillipa opened the chamber doors. Sophia saw the collected guests. Not many from England. She'd spent most of her years since university making money rather than friends so she had few. She recognised the two wives who would have lost their husbands at sea had it not been for Laurent's intervention. And some of the tenants of the Chateau's vineyards stood in their Sunday best. Jacques and Charlotte from Africa caught her attention.

The mayor in his blue, white and red sash stood behind a massive desk and an enormous Gallic moustache. And there stood Laurent in a smart suit and a big smile that sent butterflies round and round her tummy. Her dreams were about to come true.

And then she hesitated. All these people depending on Laurent what are they thinking? Do they hate me? Even with Laurent's architect earnings and my input so many will be worse off. I *am* selfish. This is wrong. And she turned and fled.

Sophia didn't respond to Phillipa's banging on the toilet door. Only her sobs could be heard. A small crowd gathered in the corridor. Laurent eased his way through.

"Sophia, what is the matter my love?"

Sophia sobbed, "I can't let you do this. Your title opens doors so you can help people. You won't ever earn enough to fill the gap between your architect's income and the chateau's. It will come between us eventually. I can't let you do this. I love you too much."

"Please, Sophia. I know what I am doing. I love you."

"And with me around you will never find someone… someone nice who will give you a legitimate heir. I must go home. Really Laurent, it's for the best."

"Please," pleaded Laurent. "Come out."

But Sophia wouldn't come out.

Laurent turned to the guests. "Please, could you wait outside?" The guests moved away slowly looking over their shoulders to see if Sophia would come out.

Sophia called, "Laurent, please, would you go too."

"I'll just be outside." Laurent turned and sadly walked away with a heavy heart.

Fifteen minutes later Sophia managed to compose herself enough to come out of the toilet. Phillipa still waited like the good friend she was. "I shouldn't have let it get this far," said Sophia.

Phillipa put her hand around Sophia's shoulder then let go again when she felt a buzz in her pocket. She lifted out Sophia's phone. The screen had 'Charlie the Rat' calling. "It's Charlie."

"He's the last person I want to talk to at the moment. No, wait a minute. I need to shout at someone and he's perfect for that."

Sophia took the phone and tapped the green button. "Sophia? It's Charlie."

"Someone called you to tell you what happened? You gloating?" she spat.

"What? Don't know what you're talking about. Look, that research. I've done my best and I'm afraid the covenant would stand up in court. I tried the Human Rights Act and every other thing I could think of, but they've got you by the short and curlies girl. I even had the covenant retranslated by an Oxford don just to make sure I'd got it right. I'm sorry."

"It's taken you long enough," she hissed.

"You have Scottish grandparents on your father's side and an Irish grandfather on your mother's side. I made some inquiries. Maybe we could get you Irish or Scottish nationality."

Sophia suddenly clutched at the straw. "Then Laurent wouldn't be marrying an Englishwoman?"

"That's right. But that's why I contacted the Oxford Don. He double-checked the covenant. It definitely says 'English born' not English nationality. That's because nationality wasn't too precise in those days. It's the English 'born' that's the problem."

"You raised my hopes there. Are you trying to upset me even further?"

"Well you probably think I'm an asshole but…"

"There's no 'probably' about it."

"Charming! Look I'm the best lawyer there is and I don't give up easily so I made some other inquiries."

"What inquiries?" said Sophia using the phone call to direct her anger at Charlie the Rat and keep her from thinking about what may have been.

"You remember that holiday we had up in Northumberland?"

"Yes." Sophia gave out a loud snort of contempt.

"And you showed me where you born, in that old barn?"

"Yes. And you fell in the stream. Pity you didn't drown."

"So I went up there to check it out," he said ignoring the jibe. "That's what's taken me so long. I found the policewoman who delivered you. She's retired and in her sixties but she remembers it well. We went to the barn," he said in his lawyer's tone.

"I'm sure you had a lovely time. Isn't she a little old for you?"

"Sophia, I know how much you detest me and to be honest you have every right. But I wanted to do something for you to make amends and that is what I've done. Your birth certificate says you are English. Your birth is registered in England. Even your parents think you were born in England."

"Yes, I know! That's the bloody problem you fool."

Charlie carried on unperturbed. "The stream your pregnant mother crossed to the barn, the stream I fell in, I've checked with Ordnance Survey, Land Registry and Google. It's the border between Scotland and England. You're not English born. You're Scots born and I have an affidavit from the policewoman to prove it."

Phillipa grabbed Sophia and the phone as they were about to tumble.

Sophia managed to speak into the phone. "Charlie thanks. We're quits and, well I just don't know how to thank you enough. Charlie, thank you thank you thank you." She pressed the red button.

At that moment Laurent, head down and hands in pockets, ambled along the corridor. He looked up at Sophia with sadness in his blue eyes.

"Can a girl change her mind twice?" said Sophia.

"You mean…" Laurent's face suddenly bursting into happiness.

"I mean I really do want to marry you if you will still have me."

He engulfed her in his arms while Phillipa dashed off to get the guests back.

Sophia would tell him the good news just as soon as she got her breath back.

The End

Printed in Great Britain
by Amazon

85497288R00088